# Chase
## And the Spirits of the Trestle
By
## KG Wauthier

# Chase And The Spirits of The Trestle

K G Wauthier

Published by K G Wauthier, 2024.

This is a work of fiction. Similarities to real people, places, or events are entirely coincidental.

CHASE AND THE SPIRITS OF THE TRESTLE

**First edition. October 11, 2024.**

Copyright © 2024 K G Wauthier.

ISBN: 979-8227206718

Written by K G Wauthier.

# Also by K G Wauthier

**The Greatest Games Series with Jake & Matti**
The Greatest Softball Game

**Standalone**
Chase And The Spirits of The Trestle

Watch for more at https://books2read.com/greatestgame.

# Table of Contents


Chase And The Spirits of The Trestle..............................................1

Chapter 1 | The Game ......................................................3

Chapter 2 | The Move........................................................7

Chapter 3 | The Fort ........................................................11

Chapter 4 | The Discovery..............................................19

Chapter 5 | Miscommunication .....................................29

Chapter 6 | The Facts of Life........................................49

Chapter 7 | Raptors and Rum.......................................55

Chapter 8 | Penance ........................................................71

Chapter 9 | The Crab Feast............................................79

Chase and the Spirits of the Trestle is based on actual events. The names have been changed to protect the innocent ... and the not-so-innocent. Some dramatizations may have been added here and there, and a bit of poetic license can't be ruled out, either.
I would like to extend my thanks to the editors of this project:
The men and women of the Withlacoochee Area Writers Association,
and
Mary Lu Scholl
Paula J Braley
and
My beautiful wife, Wanda, for all the encouragement she provided.

# Chapter 1
# The Game

It was bittersweet that summer of 1961. When July ended, so did Chase's last year of Little League baseball eligibility. He made the all-star team, but in the game, pitting the American and National leagues against one another, he was used sparingly. Chase entered the game to relieve the first-string catcher as his team took the field in the top of the final inning and trailed by one run. By the time the opposing team's best hitter came to the plate, there were two outs, runners on first and third, but no one had scored.

Chase called time out and walked toward the dugout to confer with the coach. "Can we intentionally walk this guy?"

"No. We can't do that. I'm not sure there's a rule against it, but this is an all-star game. We need to pitch to him."

The first string catcher, Craig Nolan, overheard the conversation. "I know him. That's Guy McTheison. Keep the ball inside and low. Anywhere else, and he'll knock it outta the park."

Chase trotted to the mound from the dugout to confer with Vince, their pitcher, another twelve-year-old he'd caught throughout the season with his team. "Craig says we gotta pitch this guy inside a low. I'm gonna keep the target outside-a-the strike zone 'cause walkin' him's better'n him hittin' a homer. Okay?"

"Sounds like a plan. Let's hope it works. I won't give him anything worth hittin.'"

With a smile, Chase handed Vince the ball and trotted back toward the plate.

Before pulling his mask over his face, Chase greeted the batter, "Hey," before crouching close behind him, crowding as much as he dared—one of his common tactics. Once, in a game during the regular season, a frustrated batter swung hard at a pitch that, if hit, probably would have gone over the fence. Chase saw the pitcher had *laid one up,* so he extended his mitt enough that it interfered with the batter's swing. He was crowding him so tightly that the bat hit the catcher's mitt instead of the ball. The batter was furious. The umpire called interference and warned Chase to "give the batter more room" but called it a "no pitch." Neither a ball nor a strike.

Chase was proud of himself for saving a home run.

Vince delivered his first pitch to Guy. It was inside and very close to the batter's knee.

Guy didn't flinch—stared at Vince instead.

The umpire called it. "Ball. Inside."

Chase checked the runners on base, threw the ball back to the pitcher, and yelled, "Alright, guys. Remember, two down, play's at first or second." He took up position and set his target low and inside.

Vince wound up and delivered a fastball right where Chase wanted.

"Ball two. Low," yelled the ump.

Chase tossed the ball back to the pitcher and gave him the same target once again.

Vince delivered another fastball.

"Ball three. Inside and low."

Chase stepped in front of the plate, threw the ball back hard, and yelled, "Okay, Vince. Bear down now."

As he turned, he saw Guy give him a nod. "Mm, mmm."

"What's that supposed to mean?"

"Nothin.'"

Chase crouched, set up the target, and gave him the sign for another fastball.

Vince began his windup.

Guy stepped back slightly and said, "So y'all wanna play golf, huh?"

The ball was coming inside, just like he expected, less than a foot off the ground. It was certainly out of the strike zone and going to be called a ball for sure. Guy would have been given a *walk* to first base. Instead, he took a mighty swing that resembled Ben Hogan. The ball took flight like something Chase had never seen before. He ripped off his mask in awe and watched the ball as it continued to climb and clear the lights in centerfield. Suddenly, his team trailed by four, and the inning wasn't over.

# Chapter 2
# The Move

It all came rushing back, the emotional trauma Chase struggled through being moved clear across the county from his best friend, Bill, earlier that year. They didn't attend the same school. Chase was raised Catholic, and his mother insisted that her children be brought up and educated in the church.

He remembered waving to his best friend as they pulled away with their last load of furniture. With tears in his eyes, he leaned from the back seat with his head out the window, yelling, "Bye, Bill. See ya' later."

His mother could hear the pain in his voice. "We're only moving across town, honey."

As far as Chase was concerned, they might as well have been moving to another state! He knew Bill, being a year older, was no longer eligible to play in Little League baseball. He felt more alone than ever. *We'll probably never see each other again.*

THE FAMILY HAD MOVED to a bigger home, but Chase still had to share a room with his younger half-brother. His two younger half-sisters shared an adjacent room. With adolescence setting in, he began feeling more and more like the odd man out. He was the only one who wasn't a *full* family member—the only one with a *stepdad*. To him, it was clear he was being treated differently.

It was as if a new chapter was being written in his life, and he wasn't sure he liked it. About to turn thirteen, Chase soon made new friends, Don and Mike. Since his new home bordered a vast wilderness, they spent their time exploring the woods together. After being drenched by afternoon showers on so many occasions, they talked about building a shelter.

Chase suggested, "We can cut some palm fronds and build it like the Indians did in the old days."

Don, a year-and-a-half older, scoffed. "There's houses goin' up on the other side of the subdivision. Why don't we go over there and see if there's anything they're throwin' away that we can use? You know, boards and stuff."

Mike agreed. "Great idea."

Don said, "We should ride over there and check things out."

Chase looked at him like he had two heads. A large drainage ditch separated the two sections of the subdivision. To go by road to the bridge that crossed the ditch was a fifteen-minute bike ride. "Why in the world would we do that? All that commotion sounds like it's happenin' right through there, across that damn ditch, through them woods. If we ride our bikes, it'll take ferever."

Don, the wisest of the group, let out a deep sigh. "If we go trompin' though the woods, all wet and muddy from wadin' through that *damned ditch*, and show up at them houses, we're gonna look suspicious—like we're up to no good. But three boys ridin' around on bikes is as *normal* as it gits."

They would set out on their "recon mission," as Don put it, after the workers left for the day. The homes being built were near the same patch of woods where they wanted to construct their *fort*.

Fortunately for the young *architects*, two houses were still in the framing stage, and they backed up to the drainage ditch with a wooded area left as a buffer in between.

Chase had a pretty good sense of direction and couldn't contain his excitement. "This is perfect!" He pointed toward the woods. "My house is right through there." He shifted his point to his left. "And over there is where we're gonna build our fort."

Don nodded. "I know."

Seeing a large section of plywood in the trash pile, he continued. "Look. We can use that. Let's drag it into the woods there."

Chase ran over, lifted it, and said, "This is nearly half a sheet. Heck, yeah, we can use it. I can't believe they're throwin' it away. And look at all this other stuff!"

Digging through the discarded materials, they found a trove of goodies they managed to pull into the woods.

On the ride back, Mike hollered, "We're gonna need some tools."

The thought resonated in their minds as they all nodded in agreement.

Pedaling as fast as they could, the boys hurried to their side of the woods, dropped their bikes, and ran to the bank of the drainage ditch. Despite being built for flood control, suddenly, this obstacle appeared to the young adventurers as wide and deep as the Amazon River.

The three boys stood on the high bank staring at the water flowing some eight feet below them until Chase asked, "How we gonna get that stuff over here?"

Don chuckled. "One of us is gonna wade across and toss it, piece by piece, to the others. That's how."

Mike finally broke the silence. "Who's gonna do the wadin'? Should we draw straws?"

With a hard bump from Don's shoulder, Mike tumbled down the bank. He didn't stop until he hit the water and heard, "You're already wet. Why don't you go?"

Climbing to his feet, Mike yelled, "You son-of-a-bitch! You know there's water moccasins in this ditch. You coulda threw me right on top of a damned *cottonmouth*!"

"Yeah. Coulda. I guess we just got lucky." Don pointed. "Now climb up there and start tossing stuff over here."

Looking at Chase, Don said, "Go down there, get what he throws over, and hand it up to me. I'll carry it to the job site."

Chase chuckled. "Yes, sir, boss."

"You need help getting down, or do you want a push?"

Raising his hands to signal his compliance, Chase quickly responded, "I'm good," and began his descent.

It wasn't long before they had their cache safely piled where they wanted. Don took the lead, propping boards and demonstrating his vision of how the fort might look. "We're gonna need a bunch more stuff, but it's too late today to make another run. Besides, we need to start gatherin' tools. I can sneak my dad's handsaw, but we're gonna need hammers, screwdrivers, and maybe a hatchet or a machete. Can either of you borrow some things from your parents' workshops?"

# Chapter 3
# The Fort

Over the next couple of weeks, the boys built a fort that would have been the envy of the neighborhood. Of course, it was so deep into the woods that no one could possibly know of its whereabouts. But if they had seen it, they would have been jealous.

Their construction skills may have been a bit lacking. Even with the codes in place in 1961, they never would have had a chance with a building inspector. Nonetheless, the fort did offer reasonable protection from showers. They fashioned the roof mostly out of plywood and used Chase's idea of covering it with overlapping palm fronds in place of shingles. It required considerable maintenance and was never watertight, but it provided shelter.

About the time they had it finished, they realized the rainy season was nearing an end. The expected daily showers didn't come as regularly. It was hot in Florida during the waning days of August, and the fort provided a cool, shady resting spot while recovering from their mischievous adventures. With the start of the school year looming, their lust for exploration grew.

One day, deeper in the woods than they had ever ventured, they came upon a railroad track.

Chase remarked, "I thought I heard a train whistle a few days ago."

Don's head spun. "Dumbass. You don't remember crossing the tracks every time your folks take you someplace outside the subdivision? It's just a mile or so down the road from the entrance. This must be where those tracks lead."

"Oh. Yeah. Must be." Chase was red-faced with embarrassment.

Mike giggled.

Chase punched him in the shoulder. "Shut up, Mike."

Of course, they had to follow the tracks. They were boys, after all. They walked until they came to a trestle, crossing a beautiful, crystal-clear creek.

They hurried down the steep bank to find an abundance of fish swimming everywhere.

Chase loved to fish but never got the chance to go unless his grandmother took him, and she was only here during the winter. He saw an opportunity. "Man. We gotta bring our fishin' poles and catch some of these."

Don replied, "Yeah. And bring a fryin' pan and stuff, too. We'll cook and eat 'em right here on the bank."

Mike chimed in, "Great idea."

THE FOLLOWING MORNING, the boys met at Chase's to prepare for their adventure. They decided to ride their bikes to see if they could find a shortcut to the trestle instead of hiking through the woods. It was a long walk, and it took forever to get there on foot.

Don used to deliver papers to earn extra money. He still had that colossal canvas bag they gave him to carry big bundles over his shoulder. They used that and loaded it with gear including, but not limited to, a skillet, a spatula, a can of Crisco, and a large kitchen knife.

When Chase put his tackle box and a frozen package wrapped in newspaper into the bag, his eyes widened.

"That's a mighty big knife for cleanin' fish, Don."

"We're gonna need that for a lot more'n cleanin' fish. What's in the wrapper, yer lunch?"

"Nope. That's our bait. Gramma and I got rained out the last time we went fishin' before she and Grandpa went back up north. We had some frozen shrimp left over, and I talked Mom into lettin' me put it back in the freezer so I could keep it. She'd only let me if I wrapped it real good in newspaper. Hope it'll still work."

"You are stupid, ain't ya?"

"What are you talkin' about?"

"Shrimps live in *salt*water. That creek's gotta be *fresh* water. Those fish ain't never tasted a shrimp. We ain't gonna catch a single fish on them things."

Don and Mike started laughing like fools, bent over double and slapping their knees. Embarrassed again, Chase felt awful. "We'll see." *I sure hope they're wrong. Maybe when the fish smell 'em, they'll take a bite to see what it tastes like.*

With all they thought they needed stowed in the bag, Don put the strap over his head so it hung over one shoulder and attempted to mount his new, fancy, English racer bicycle. It wasn't a good fit. The bag hung too low, and when he leaned to reach the handlebars, it slid up on his neck. Don tried running both arms through, wearing it like a backpack, but the load contacted the back tire, and the bike had no fenders. This would not do. The strap was too long.

Chase's mother, watching from the window, stepped out and suggested, "Why don't you tie a knot in the strap?"

The boys looked puzzled. She motioned with her hand. "Tie a knot in it. It'll make the strap shorter and keep it off your tire." She was eager to get the boys out of her carport.

Don finally got the idea, tied the knot, and it worked. "Thanks, Mrs. Kean."

Smiling, she replied, "You're welcome," and closed the door.

Mike didn't have a fishin' pole, so Don handed him his. "Here. You've got a free hand. Carry mine. And *don't break it.*"

Off they headed. Don led the way, followed by Chase. Mike brought up the rear. Not used to handling a fishing rod and not wanting to miss anything said between the boys in front, Mike tended to stay closer than he should have, considering he was carrying a six-and-a-half-foot fishing rod in his right hand along with the handlebars.

Sure enough, when he wasn't paying attention, the tip of the rod caught in the spokes of Chase's rear wheel. The force of it jerked the rod from Mike's fingers, and it fell to the pavement, where it bounced along until Chase realized something was wrong and stopped his bike.

In horror, Mike slammed on his brakes, dropped his bike, and ran for his life.

Don laid his ride gently on the ground, looked at the carnage of what used to be his only fishin' pole, and yelled, "Mike, I'm gonna *kill* you! I gave you *one* job."

Taking his anger out on Chase, he said, "Why didn't you stop quicker?"

"Hey. I didn't even know what happened. I did the best I could. I stopped as soon as I heard the noise."

"Bullshit. He's *yer* friend anyway, so this is *yer* fault. You owe me a new fishin' pole."

"Hey, yer the one who gave him the job of carryin' the thing. Not me."

"Yeah. Dumb move on my part." Examining the situation more closely, Don continued. "Look at this mess. There's fishin' line wrapped around your wheel. How we gonna get my rod outta there—all these busted pieces of fiberglass? Shiiiittt."

Once they cut the line, things got easier. Sadly, Don's rod had lost over a foot of its length, the reel was banged up from road abrasion, and its handle was bent but still rotated. They weren't sure if they'd see Mike again—ever—so they pulled his bike from the roadway and left it. They pushed on toward their destination.

They finally reached the point where the tracks crossed the road. Here, they would ditch their bikes safely away from the pavement, unnoticeable to passersby, and make it the rest of the way on foot.

Eagerly, they hurried down to the water's edge.

Once again, Chase was ecstatic. "Man, look at these fish! They're everywhere, and they look *hungry*."

"Holy crap. Since you're the only one with a working fishin' pole, you start *catchin'* some. I'll cut some firewood."

"Okay." Chase unwrapped his frozen shrimp, put a small piece on his hook, and dropped the line into the water. Much to his disappointment, nary a fish gave it a single look. It was ignored as if it didn't exist until a handsome blue crab emerged from under a log, grabbed the hook with one of his pinchers, and began to dine.

Chase lifted his rod tip, figuring the crab would let go. Evidently, the crustacean was particularly hungry. Holding on until dangling nearly two feet above the water, he finally turned loose and swam back to safety.

Chase examined the piece of shrimp on his hook, adjusted it to ensure its security, and dropped his line back into the water.

He held the bait, perhaps a foot beneath the water's surface, to watch the fish. Several showed up to investigate. They circled the strange hunk of unfamiliar flesh but didn't know what to do. Then, a small fish, too tiny to eat it, came up and bumped the bait before quickly backing off to see what might happen next.

Chase was fascinated, hoping a big one would emerge from hiding under a log or in the grass to swallow the shrimp. *Surely, these little fish'll pique a biggun's interest.*

Don walked up carrying an armload of small pieces of wood they could use to build a fire. "What the hell are you doin'?"

"Tryin' to attract a biggin to come out from his hidin' spot."

"Is that so?"

"Yeah. Look at all these lil'uns checkin' out this bait."

"Uh, huh. Any of 'em taken a bite of it yet?"

"No. None of 'em's big enough. But check this out." Chase dropped the bait to the bottom, and *three* blue crabs scurried out, fighting to see who got there first.

Don couldn't believe his eyes. "Holy crap!"

Once Chase was comfortable at least one of the crabs had a good hold on the bait, he gently lifted the rod tip. Two of them held on until they were out of the water before letting go.

"Oh, man. We should have brought a *pot* instead of a skillet! A pot and a net. You lift 'em up, and I'll slide a net under 'em. We'll catch a *mess* of those guys."

Don was excited. He decided to cut a few small limbs off a nearby sapling hanging over the creek. Placing his left hand to steady himself to reach a limb that needed trimming, Don swung the large chef's knife. Somehow, he hit his hand in addition to the tree, resulting in a gash between his thumb and forefinger. Blood shot everywhere.

"Holy shit! I cut myself."

"Oh, no! What are we gonna do?"

"I don't know!" Clutching his hand with blood spilling from the wound, Don was frantic.

"Here, help me get this T-shirt off me. I'll use it as a bandage. Hell, it's all we got. Maybe it'll stop the bleedin.'"

Chase helped as best he could despite Don being considerably taller. Confusion reigned. Don bent over at the waist, and Chase pulled. The shirt came off.

Don wrapped it as tight as he could around his blood-soaked hand. Running to his bike, he said, "C'mon. We gotta go. This is prob'ly gonna need some stitches."

They left all their things on the creekbank and hightailed it for home.

On the way, Chase noticed Mike's bike was gone. *He must have been scared to death Don was gonna pound him.*

SUSPICION FLASHED WHEN she saw her son ride up. She stepped into the carport and said, "Chase. What are you doing home already?"

"Don cut his thumb, so we had to come back early. It was bleedin' pretty bad."

"Is he okay?"

"Yeah. I guess. It looked like it quit bleedin' by the time we got here. He didn't look like he was dyin' or nothin' like that."

"How did he do it?"

"He was cuttin' a stick with his knife. I guess it musta slipped or sump'in. Or else he wasn't payin' attention."

"Where's all your stuff?"

"He was pretty scared, so we left it all there and hurried home."

"Aren't you afraid someone'll come along and steal it while you're gone?"

"Naw. Ain't nobody knows where that place is, Mom. B'sides, we'll be back there tomorra.'"

"I think I should call Don's mother."

"Maybe, but she's prob'ly takin' him to the doctor already. She won't be home to answer. Don said he figured it might need stitches."

"Oh, dear."

Eager to escape the inquisition, Chase asked, "Is it okay if I go over to Mike's?"

# Chapter 4
# The Discovery

At the Bifano house, Chase knocked on the door. When it opened, he said, "Hi, Mrs. B. Is Mike home?"

Wearing her apron and a cocked brow with a fist on her hip, she responded, "What's going on, Chase? Mike came flying in here over an hour ago, dripping with sweat, looking like he was running from a mafia boss."

"Who?"

"Never mind. Did you boys get into a fight or somethin'?"

"No, ma'am. Mike accidentally broke Don's fishin' pole, and he thought Don might beat the snot out of him, so he ran. That's all. I reckon Don *was* pretty mad, but he's over it now. That's why I'm here, to let him know everythin's okay, and he don't have to worry none."

"I figured something happened, but Mike wouldn't spill the beans. He's in his room." She turned to head toward the kitchen before adding, "Probably still lickin' his wounds."

"Thanks, Mrs. B." Chase headed down the hall to the bedroom, where he filled his friend in on all the gory details.

With all the pent-up excitement he'd been keeping bottled up inside, Chase let it all out. "Man, you shoulda seen it when he hit his hand with that humongous knife a his. Blood squirted out like a fire hose!

"Don dropped that knife, screamed like a baby, and grabbed it with his other'n to try to stop the bleedin'. It didn't help much.

"Then he told me to pull his T-shirt off him so he could wrap his hand up in it, hoping it would work like a bandage. We rode home as fast as we could. By the time we got here, that T-shirt was drippin' wet with blood." Chase shook his head.

"It was bad. He's prob'ly still at the doctor's office. No tellin' how many stitches it's gonna take."

In case his mom might be listening through the door, Mike whispered, "No shit? I wish I'da stuck around."

"I bet. But we left in such a hurry, all our stuff is still layin' right there on the creek bank. You wanna ride over there with me and git it?"

THEY ARRIVED AT THE creek, and Chase couldn't wait to show Mike the scene of the carnage and describe the events one more time. "You shoulda seen it, Man. Blood was flyin' everywhere!" He pointed, "Look. Here, and here. And over here. Don was scared as shit."

"Holy cow. I bet he *was* scared. I'm glad I wasn't here. I prob'ly woulda throwed up."

Chase sighed. "Yeah. Prob'ly fer the best."

Chase found his now-thawed shrimp lying on the sandy bank, swarming with tiny, black bugs. As he reached for a piece of bait, his friend asked, "What are those things, ants, tiny beetles, or sump'n else?"

"Naw, they's shrimp. They was frozen, but not anymore."

"I'm not talkin' about whatever that is. I'm talkin' about what's crawlin' on top."

"I dunno. But once I drop it in the water, I 'spect they'll wash off, so it don't matter none," Chase chuckled as he carefully slid a piece onto his hook.

"Eeww! I can't believe yer touchin' that. Aren't you afraid they're gonna bite you or pinch you? Maybe they have stingers. Heck, they could be poisonous!"

Chase dropped the bait into the water, rubbed his fingers in the sand to remove the slime, and said, "Naw. Them shrimps are dead. You worry too much, Mike. Now watch."

As soon as the bait got near the bottom, the blue crabs came a-runnin'. Mike couldn't believe his eyes. "Holy schmolly. What *are* those?"

"Them's blue crabs, baby. My grandpa and I go fishin' for 'em when he comes down for the winter, 'cept we use a trap and go out into the bay. Never seen 'em in freshwater b'fore, but here they are. When Don gets better, we're gonna bring a big pot and a net, catch a bunch, boil 'em right here, and have a feast."

"A net? How does that work?"

"Here. Watch. I'll lift 'em up like this ..." Chase slowly lifted his rod tip, "... and one a y'all just slide a net underneath. When the crab lets go, ya' got 'em. Easy, right?"

With the crab slightly above the water line, Chase swung his rod slowly toward the bank. The crustacean hung on until it nearly reached the shore before letting go.

Mike's excitement was written all over him. "That's awesome! Where we gonna get a pot and net? You know my mom ain't gonna let me take one a her pots outta the house, and we both know my dad dern sure doesn't have a net."

"Yeah. I don't reckon mine will, either. The way Don was talkin' though, I got the feelin' he could get 'em. I'm hopin' so.

"Hey. Let's hide this stuff over in the bushes and walk across the creek up on the trestle. Want to?"

Hesitantly, Mike agreed. "O ... kay."

The boys hurried up the bank to the tracks, walking between the rails, stepping from one tie to the next with granite stones in between.

Until that is, they reached where the roadbed ended and trestle began. Suddenly, their resolve waned.

Standing side by side, looking at the openness under their feet, Mike said, "I guess I didn't realize it was so high, and I could see the creek by looking straight down. What if a train comes?"

Chase was naturally afraid of heights. That was *not* what he needed to hear. Of the two, he was far more fearless than Mike and wanted to be more like Don—not afraid of anything. Chase swallowed hard. "The train ain't comin'. Come on, don't look down."

With great trepidation, Chase led the way. He stepped out onto the first tie not fully encased in those comforting granite rocks. *That was easy enough.*

He took another step. Then, two more. Suddenly, he sensed Mike wasn't right behind him. He turned to see. His suspicion confirmed, he asked, "You comin'?"

"I think I hear the train."

"Are you serious?"

Mike nodded aggressively. "Yeah. It's way off, but I hear it!"

"If you put your ear to the rail, you'll be able to hear for sure."

"Really?" Mike responded before dropping to his knees. "What should I be listening for?"

"Yer prob'ly gonna hear there ain't no train, dumbass. Yer just chicken."

Just then, a breeze swept up the creek. Not particularly strong, but enough to make Chase stretch his arms out to his sides and bend his knees for balance. With Mike standing back on terra firma, the improbable—but still possible—approaching train, and the *hurricane* that mysteriously appeared out of nowhere, Chase's courage scurried off.

Doing an about-face on the railroad tie that had suddenly, in Chase's mind's eye, shrunk to the size of a two-by-four, he said, "I think I hear that train, too, Mike. Maybe we should try this another time."

Following the tracks back toward their bikes, Mike looked down to his right. The opposite side from where they had been focusing their attention fishing. Pointing, he said, "What's all that stuff?"

Chase stepped over so he could see. "What *is* that?" They ran down the rocky slope to the pile of bottles, many broken, but some not, dumped beside the tracks.

Rifling through the cache, Chase said, "These are, or used to be liquor bottles, and they got tags on 'em. This one says 'Magistrate Court. Salty's Tavern.' What's that one say?"

"Looks like they all say that. Whaddya think these tags are for, Chase?"

"Dunno, but it looks like Salty's is in some kinda trouble. I wonder why they got dumped way out here."

The boys continued to pick through the broken glass until Chase came across something that caught his eye. "Hey, look, *Seagram's 7*. I think this is what my stepdad drinks and it ain't broke. It ain't never been opened either." Holding it up for his friend to see, he pointed with his finger. "Look here. The paper seal over the top ain't even tore."

BRIGHT AND EARLY THE following morning, Don showed up at Chase's house carrying a large cooking pot and a landing net. Standing in the carport, he knocked on the door that opened into the kitchen. He could see Chase's mom through the open jalousie panes. She was at the sink washing the breakfast dishes.

Without leaving her duties, she turned and saw his bandage. "How's your hand, Don?"

"Oh, it's fine, Mrs. Keane. Kinda sore. I guess it looked a lot worse than it was. Only took a *few* stitches. Sure was a lotta blood, though."

"I'll bet it scared you, huh? Chase said it bled clear through your T-shirt."

"Yes, ma'am. Is he here?"

"Yeah. I hear him coming. He should be here any second."

Her son ran past her before she finished the sentence. "Bye, Mom."

"You boys have a good time. But be more careful today. Please."

As the door closed, Don pointed toward his friend's bike and said, "I'm glad to see you brought my bag from the creek where we left it." Lifting the items he was carrying, he continued. "We can use it to haul *these* things. Let's go get Mike. I need to tell him I'm not gonna kill him."

"I already told him that, but yeah, let's go. We've got somethin' to show ya' at the fort."

"What?"

"You'll see."

WITH MIKE IN TOW, THEY made their way through the woods. "Why are we stopping here? We need to be catching some of them crabs, damn it."

Chase insisted. "No. You gotta see this first. Then we'll go crabbin.'"

Finally, Don said, "Okay. So, what's the big deal?"

Mike was beaming with pride at his discovery. With his arms folded across his chest, he nodded toward the fort's entrance. "Why don't you look inside and check out what we found on the *other* side of the trestle."

Don ducked through the opening, let his eyes adjust to the dim light, and saw a half-dozen liquor bottles lined up against the wall. "What the hell is this? You found these next to those railroad tracks? Are there more?"

Don picked up each and examined them, one by one. "None of these have been opened! This is amazing. Let's go!"

AT THE TRESTLE, THEY combed through their find and scored dozens more of various sizes. After filling the bag, Don realized it had become too heavy. "There's no way I can carry this many. We'll have to make another trip or two."

After removing several bottles, Don ran his arms through the strap and climbed onto his bike. When he leaned over, the bag draped clumsily, and with his sore hand, it was impossible. He said, "If you guys lift two more bottles out of each side at the same time, that might be enough. Let's try that. Okay?"

The boys agreed, and it worked.

WHEN THEY REACHED THE fort, they added the bottles to the ones along the wall and hurried back for another load.

They had to start a second row to finish lining up this group. They had run out of walls. It was too late to make another run, so the boys leaned back on their elbows to admire their work.

Hot and sweaty, they were astonished at their accomplishment. They exchanged smiles and couldn't resist the temptation to have their first taste of this magic, forbidden elixir that was about to change their lives forever. Don asked, "What should we try first, fellas?"

Mike shrugged his shoulders. "I dunno what any of 'em taste like."

Of course, Chase didn't either. "All I know is my stepdad drinks that *Seagrams 7* stuff. When we go to the Moose Lodge, I hear him order, 'Seven and Seven, please.' So, that must be it. Right? I guess it must be good. Huh?"

Don was slightly more experienced than the other two boys but still had no clue. "Okay. Let's try that one, then. I have an idea." He opened the bottle of *Seagrams* and removed the cap from two others. He poured a little whiskey into the three caps so each boy had what he *thought* was a tiny sip. "Now, don't taste or smell it until we can all do it together. Okay?"

They all cautiously drew the potent liquid close to their mouths as if they were somehow connected and moved as one. Don resumed his instructions. "Ready. Go."

The tears, coughs, gasps, screams, and one cry seemed to go on forever. It's unclear who said it, but a voice rang out. "How can grown-ups drink this shit?"

Astonished and frustrated, the boys dumped whatever remained in their respective caps. Don reinstalled them on their appropriate containers, and the boys went home, venting their ire as they trekked through the woods until Don finally asked, "Chase. What did you say your stepdad orders at the Moose Lodge?"

"Seven and Seven. Why?"

"Well, I'm wonderin' if adults *mix* that stuff with somethin' else, maybe it wouldn't taste so bad. Maybe 'Seven and Seven' means what we drank is mixed with '7-up'. That might change everything. Right?"

It was like a lightbulb turned on in Chase's brain. "Hey, today's Saturday. We'll probably be going to the Moose tonight. I'll pay attention when they order their drinks and maybe ask more questions. See what I can find out."

Don nodded. "Perfect."

Mike followed along, seemingly oblivious to the entire conversation.

THE WAITRESS AT THE Moose Lodge arrived with the adult beverages and placed them accordingly. "Here ya go, Walt." She smiled, adding, "And a Sloe Gin Fizz for you, Doris. I love those things. I tried one the other day because you order them all the time. They taste as good as they look. So pretty. Y'all ready to order?"

Doris chuckled, "No. Give us a few minutes to figure out what everybody wants. Okay?"

"Sure 'nuff, honey. Take your time. I'll be back."

Chase seized the opportunity. "What is that you ordered, Mom? It *is* pretty."

Doris cocked her head, looked at the glass, and gave it a stir. "Yeah, it is. Isn't it? It's made with Sloe Gin, but I'm not sure what else goes into it. Do you know, Walt?"

Appearing annoyed with the question, he said, "Sugarwater and soda's about all I know. Who cares about those sissy drinks? Y'all better be decidin' what ya wanna eat."

With a confused look, Chase asked, "*Slow* gin? Is there a *fast* gin? Are they differ'nt?"

Walt laughed, nearly choking on his drink.

Doris smiled. "No. It's Sloe, spelled s-l-o-e. I think it's made from a berry that grows somewhere in the world. I think that's where it gets its red color."

"I've never heard of a 'Sloe berry,' Mom. How did it get its name?"

"I have no idea about that one, Son."

"That's weird."

"I can't disagree, Chase."

Walt was getting anxious. "Are we gonna order or not? I'm starving."

"Yes, dear. As soon as our waitress comes back." Turning her attention to the other children, she asked, "Do you all know what you want?"

A chorus of absurd hopes and wishes were debated until it was clear they would have what Momma decided. Doris allowed some latitude but was a master at guiding the children's decision-making.

The watchful waitress showed up and took their food order. After she walked away, Chase asked his stepfather, whom he *never* called *dad*, "So, Walt. You don't like 'sissy drinks.' Right? What's 'Seven and Seven'?"

His stepdad couldn't help but chuckle. "What's with the questions about adult drinks all of a sudden?"

"I dunno. It's just these words I've never heard before. Got me wonderin', that's all."

"Well, a 'Seven and Seven' is whiskey and '7-up', if you must know."

"Oh. Does whiskey taste good?"

"It has a distinct flavor, but it's pretty strong. Some people drink it straight, but most mix it like I do—with water, 7-up, Coke, things like that. But, of course, whiskey is only for adults over twenty-one. Remember that. Okay?"

"Oh. Fer sure."

IN THEIR BEDROOM, DORIS was changing into her pajamas. "Walt. Did you find Chase's questions about our drinks rather strange this evening?"

"Kinda. Why?"

"They were interesting, weren't they?"

"I think he was just fascinated with your drink choice. It was pretty, the color and all the bubbles. And its name, *Sloe Gin Fizz*. I can see why he might have been prompted to ask about it."

"Maybe. Call me a worry-wort if you will, but I've got my antenna up. I'll keep my eye on him."

"You do that, Honey. I've given up on figurin' out that boy of yours, especially since puberty started settin' in."

"Don't remind me. Let's go to bed."

# Chapter 5

# Miscommunication

When they got home from church, Chase changed clothes and hurried to Don's. He was eager to share his newfound information about the liquor. When he knocked on the door, his friend's mother answered. "Don has been grounded and won't be available for a week. Goodbye." Without giving him a chance to reply, she closed the door.

The young boy stood there a moment before his words came out. "Yes, ma'am."

As he turned to leave, he saw Don's black, shiny, new English racer bicycle Chase and Mike envied. It was bigger and faster than theirs. The tires were sleek and thin. *Man, I bet that thing'll fly!* He ran all the way to Mike's.

When his friend joined him outside, they walked toward the woods since Mike's bike had a flat tire. "Don's grounded."

"How do you know?"

"I stopped at his house on my way here."

"No shit? I wonder what he did."

"I don't know. His mom didn't give me a chance to ask. She *slammed* the door in my face."

"Really?"

"I'm tellin' ya true, Man. She wouldn't even let Don come to the door."

"Holy schmolly. I never thought about *him* gettin' grounded. Did you?"

"Not really. I reckon we'll find out soon enough, but wait 'till I tell you what I learned last night about whiskey."

Chase spent the rest of the walk, at least to the end of the block, speaking as though he was an aficionado of alcoholic beverages. Mike was in awe, hanging on his every word.

They spent the afternoon traipsing through the woods, chasing critters, or being bored. The subject of Don's bike kept coming up. They avoided the liquor because they lacked appropriate mixers. However, Chase surprised his friend when he proposed an idea. "We need a table for our fort."

"A table? What for?"

"B'cause we need a place to sit our glasses where we can mix the Coke with the whiskey. Or the 7-up. Whatever we decide to use. And we need some ice, too."

"Where we gonna get the money for all this stuff?"

Chase broke into a big grin. "*Improvise.*"

WHEN HE WALKED THROUGH the door, Chase's mother said, "You're home earlier than normal. What's up?"

"I'm bored. Don got in trouble."

"What for?"

"I don't know. His mom wouldn't say. She just told me he was grounded and closed the door."

"Did you see him do anything bad?"

"No. Unless she's mad 'cause he took her cookin' pot or somethin'."

"Oh. Maybe you should return it."

"*Mom.* What if that ain't what she's mad about?"

Doris chuckled. "Well, we wouldn't want to make a mistake like *that*, now would we?"

"*No.* I got no idea." He walked to his room.

After dinner, Chase asked his mother, "Is it okay if I go over to Mike's for a while?"

"Is it alright with the Bifanos?"

"Of course. Mrs. B likes me a lot, Mom."

"I suppose. Don't wear out your welcome."

"Okay. Thanks. Bye." Chase headed out the door.

When he arrived and knocked on the neighbor's door, Mike answered. After a brief conversation, Mike asked, "Mom, is it alright if Chase and I take a walk around the neighborhood?"

"It's dark out there, Mike."

"I know, Mom. We'll be fine."

"Alright. Don't you be getting into no trouble. Do you hear me?"

"We won't, Mamma. Bye."

The boys headed straight to Don's to *borrow* his new bike. Quietly, they slipped beside the house. There it was, their target, standing tall in front of the family auto parked in the carport.

Chase carefully lifted the kickstand so it wouldn't make any noise. He remembered when Don had pushed his bike backward, and it made a clicking sound. *Stupid English bikes.* He lifted the rear tire off the concrete floor to ensure its silent removal before walking it behind the adjacent house next door. From there they headed to the street where they mounted up. Chase threw his leg over the seat and steadied the bike, holding on to the handlebars where Mike could sit with the soles of his shoes on the axle bolts of the front wheel.

They knew the neighborhood streets, so everything was going well even though it was dark. That is until they turned onto a long straightaway where Chase could see how fast he could make that bike go.

The wind was whipping past his ears, making it difficult for Chase to hear his forward-facing passenger when he said, "Car."

Mike referred to a parked, dull-black, vintage 1940s-era sedan with a steeply sloped trunk lid and a simple steel bumper.

Pedaling hard, Chase said, "Huh?"

Louder, Mike said, "Car."

"What?"

This time, he yelled. "Car!"

Not letting up, Chase replied, "I can't hear—"

IT'S UNCLEAR WHETHER it was the pop of the front tire when it blew and the rim twisted into a figure-eight, the crunch of the impact, bicycle against bumper, or the thud of Chase's body hitting the car's roof just above the rear window. Perhaps it was the tinny sound, like a poorly tuned gong, when Mike landed on the hood of the old Plymouth, followed by the whines and moans of both boys trying to catch their breath.

Whatever the cause, the commotion resulted in an almost immediate reaction. A light suddenly illuminated the front of the home closest to the collision, and the door flew open a split second later. A middle-aged man, who appeared to be the car's owner, came running out. Angry at first, he assessed the situation. "Are you boys okay?"

With the wind knocked out of them, neither could answer right away. Mike was trying to figure out how to climb off the hood of the man's car. Chase was looking for a way to dismount without impaling himself on the mangled bicycle ... and holding back tears.

The man reached out a hand to help Chase down from his perch. "Come on, son. How bad are you hurt?

He accepted the man's help and stepped on the old bumper to the ground. "I'm not sure. I'm sorry, mister. I surely didn't see your car."

After seeing no apparent damage to his sedan, the man chuckled. "I'm sure you didn't, young man. Let me go help your friend." He walked around to the front and offered to assist Mike, struggling to find a way down.

"Are you all right, son?"

"I think so. That was scary." He giggled awkwardly, trying to keep from crying, too.

"Did you guys not see the car?"

"I did. I kept sayin' 'Car,' but I guess he couldn't hear me."

Chase shrugged. "We musta been goin' so fast the wind was blowin' in my ears. I kept sayin' 'What? I can't hear ya.' B'fore he could say it loud enough—BAM!"

Nodding toward the car, the man said, "I have to admit, it is faded—a dull black. It don't reflect none. I'm tryin' to save enough to get it painted, but it's expensive. It's an antique, you know. I'm sorry you boy's got hurt ..." he pointed toward the mutilated mass of metal "... and tore up your bike like that. Need some help gettin' it home?"

Quickly, Chase replied, "No! We'll be fine. We live real close. Thanks anyway, though." Absorbing the carnage of Don's bicycle for the first time made him nauseous. He looked at his friend with an expression that spoke *for* him. *What are we gonna do?*

Mike took charge. "We're sorry, mister." He reached down and lifted the front end of the wreckage. In the dark, all they could tell was the front wheel was a twisted mess, and the forks were bent back, apparently past the frame. He tucked the front wheel under his arm and let the rear tire roll on the ground behind him. They headed toward home, limping as best they could, taking turns dragging the bike.

On the trip back, Chase came up with another idea. "My stepdad has this big ole' pipe wrench. If we take the front wheel off, we might be able to use that wrench to bend the forks back in place. Then, maybe we could straighten the rim and readjust the spokes so it runs true ag'in. Whaddya think?"

"Don's gonna kill us."

"So, it's worth a try then?"

"I guess. What we got to lose? One good thing. Looks like the front tire *didn't* blow out. The tube's still holdin' air. Musta made that loud noise when it popped off the rim."

Chase agreed. "That is good news."

They finally reached Chase's house and found Walt's pipe wrench and other tools. They flipped the bike upside down onto its seat and handlebars and removed the crumpled front wheel, the rim of which had warped something awful. The crash dented its edge, several spokes bent severely, and three had snapped in half. After removing the broken ones, Mike dangled a piece of one in the air. "Whadda we do about these?"

"Let's worry about straightenin' the forks first. Then we'll decide what to do about the wheel. Okay?"

Chase adjusted the wrench collar so the jaws would fit tight against an arm of the fork. With a firm grip on the long pipe wrench handle, he instructed his friend, "Hold on to the back end of the bike. I'm gonna press hard here, and it'll make that end wanna come up. Ready?"

Suddenly, the carport light came on, and Doris opened the door. "What are you boys doin' out here? Whose bike is that, Chase? Is that Don's new bike?" She placed her hand over her mouth as if in shock and stepped out to get a better look. "What have you two done?"

"It's not as bad as it looks, Mom."

"Oh, *really*? I can't wait to hear this one."

"I told you Don's grounded. Right?"

"Yes."

"Well, he got this new English racer bicycle, and he can't ride it for a whole week. Mom, it's *real* fast, and Mike's bike has a flat tire ..." Doris waited impatiently for him to finish, "... so we decided to borrow Don's."

"Did Don give you permission to *borrow* his bike?"

"Not exactly, but we *always* borrow things from each other. We do it all the time. It's no big deal. B'sides, we couldn'ta asked him anyway. His mom won't even let him come to the door."

Doris nodded. "I *see*. So, what are you doing now?"

"We kinda had a little problem."

"A *little problem*?" Pointing to their mess, she continued. "Chase, it looks like it might have been a bit more than that. What happened?"

Chase spilled the beans and told his mom the truth.

"Were you hurt?"

"Uh, *yeah*. It hurt like hell. I mean, like heck. Sorry, Mom."

Doris flashed with anger. "Do you want me to wash your mouth out with *soap*, young man?"

"No, ma'am. I'm sorry."

"So, what do you intend to do?"

"I hope we can fix it and maybe he won't notice anything ever happened."

"Oh. You think you're that good, huh?"

Chase nodded his head with confidence. "Yeah. We can fix it."

"You don't think you should just come clean, apologize, and offer to pay for the repairs out of your allowance?"

"I sure hope it don't come to *that*."

Doris chuckled. "I expect *that's* true. You boys be careful you don't do any *more* damage or hurt yourselves, and remember to put everything away when you're finished. I'll leave the light on so you can see what you're doing." She closed the door and went back inside to her TV show.

When Chase pressed down on the pipe wrench, the fork bent as he had hoped, but the shiny, black paint was hard and brittle, so it chipped off in the area of the bend near the yoke. And, of course, the teeth of the pipe wrench had bitten into the metal through the paint at the other end, where the fork would attach to the wheel.

They repeated the exercise on the second arm of the fork. Chase eyeballed, the best he could, to make them even.

With a pair of plyers, vise-grips, and a screwdriver, they kinda worked out the dent in the rim where it collided with the bumper. They loosened all the remaining spokes and straightened the bent ones to make the rim spin reasonably true again. Chase said, "Did you notice that the broken spokes are all close together? What if we move two around from other areas to fill in the gap, so there's just one missin' in three differn't places? That way, he prob'ly won't even notice there's any missin.'"

Mike shrugged. "Worth a try."

When they finished adjusting the spokes and got it back together, the front wheel remained slightly out of round, and the rim rubbed the front brake pads on every rotation. The cracked and missing paint, the scraped and gouged metal notwithstanding, the boys pushed the bike through the connecting yards to Don's house, where they parked it on its kickstand in front of his parent's car as if nothing had happened.

The gleaming new English Racer was now heavily battle-scarred and severely weakened. They would wait with their fingers crossed until Don's grounding ended or someone in his family noticed the damage.

When they woke the following morning, Doris couldn't wait to remind her children of the good news. "Rise and shine, you little bundles of joy. Today is Labor Day. I think we should do something special because it's a National holiday, and the best part is, school starts tomorrow! Yay!!!"

Chase was the first to respond. "Oh, yippee. How exciting." His words were dripping with sarcasm, and behind her back, he mocked a gag, pretending to stick a finger down his throat. His siblings snickered, drawing their mother's attention.

"Now, Chase. Don't be a smart-aleck. School should be fun."

"Maybe it *should* be, but it ain't. At least not for me anyway."

"And why is that? Your brother and sister don't seem to mind it. You get good grades. Why do you hate it so?"

"Because it's hot, dull, and boring. All the teacher does is blah, blah, blah. And the nuns! Don't get me started. It's all so useless, Mom. I'd rather be outside. I can't sit still that long. They're all drivin' me *crazy*."

"Yeah, but just think of it. This is your last year at Saint Ann's. You're going into eighth grade. You'll graduate this year. It'll be like your senior year at high school. All the other kids will look up to you."

Chase scoffed at her words. He never went to kindergarten. Because he was born in early November, his mother enrolled him in first grade when he was five, so he was one of the youngest in the class. "They will not. I'm one of the shortest kids in my grade. There's only two who even come close. Nobody looks *up* to me, Mom."

"They do. You just don't realize it, Chase. I wish you weren't always carryin' around that chip on your shoulder. Now, come on. We're gonna have a good day together. How about we go to the beach? We'll pack some sandwiches, put the top down on the convertible, and head to the water. What do you say?"

His brother and sisters squealed in anticipation. Chase finally said, "Sounds like fun, Mom. Is Walt comin' too?"

"No, you know he doesn't like the beach. Besides, he's got some work around here he needs to take care of."

"Okay. Shotgun!" Chase loved that 1959 Ford Fairlane Galaxy 500 Skyliner. Walt's business had been doing well, and he purchased it off the showroom floor as a surprise for Doris. The car was all black except for that classic silver or gold stripe down each side. On this vehicle, they were flamingo pink, Doris's favorite color. It's probably the only one of its kind.

Chase envisioned himself as Mr. Cool riding shotgun and heading to the beach in that fancy ride. The only thing better would have been if he had been driving, but he knew he was a little more than a year away from that opportunity. Still, Chase counted the days until fourteen would click over on the calendar, and his learner's permit would be attainable. He dreamed of one day inheriting the car. *I don't want them to die, but if they would only will it to me when I turn sixteen. That would be perfect.*

THEY SPENT A COUPLE of hours that afternoon at the beach. Doris lounged in the sun, reading a book while the kids splashed in the water and frolicked on the sand. Once they were exhausted, they packed up and headed home.

On the ride, the two younger siblings quickly fell asleep. The older sister did her best to stay awake leaning against the back of the front seat, eavesdropping on the conversation between mother and son when Doris said, "You know this thing about Don's bike isn't over. Right?"

Chase didn't look up. He thought about her comment for a moment before blurting out the words. "Well, I didn't see that ... car, Mom. What was I supposed to do? I nearly killed myself—and Mike."

"I know, honey. I noticed the bruises on you in your swimsuit. Does it hurt bad?"

"Yeah. I'm pretty sore."

"I'll bet you are. God has a way of teaching us lessons when we mess up. Doesn't he?"

"I guess so."

His sister snickered.

"Shut up."

"Now, Chase. That's no way to talk to your sister. Apologize."

"Mom! She had no right to laugh at me."

"True. I guess you should apologize to each other. Go on. Both of you."

In unison, they said, "Sorry."

"There. Was that so difficult? Since I guess neither of you meant it, I suppose it was a wash." She kept driving and smiled.

"So, Chase, when does Don's punishment end? When does he get ungrounded?"

"Not sure. I think, maybe Thursday."

"Okay. Well, I haven't heard from either of his parents yet. You start school tomorrow, but it's only for half a day. Wednesday is your first full day back. We'll know soon enough, I guess. How much money do you have saved up?"

"I don't know exactly. A little over a hundred dollars, I think. Why?"

"Because I suspect there's gonna be a bill coming for repairs to that bike, and I think you and Mike should split the cost. That's why."

"Really? You think that's gonna happen?"

"Of course I do. You boys *borrowed* and *damaged* the bike; therefore, you are *responsible* for it. It's only right."

Chase slumped in his seat, put his hand over his forehead, and said, "Oh, Mom."

With a sick feeling in his stomach, Chase was no longer Mr. Cool. He sat quietly for the rest of the ride home, staring off to the side of the road, pondering the end of his summer.

CHASE COULD TELL HIS stepdad was *not* in a good mood when they pulled into the driveway. He had been finishing up a task when he heard Doris pull in. He stood and began wiping his hands on the shop towel he took from his back pocket, but the expression on his face told the story.

Without moving, Walt's eyes never left Chase's as the car drew nearer. Doris finally put it in Park and opened her door. Chase was frozen. The three siblings quickly followed their mother out of the vehicle and hurried inside. Doris busied herself, gathering the blanket and other items left in the vehicle. The top was still down on the car, so Walt, in his loud, deep voice, said, "I had the opportunity to meet Mrs.

Malone, Don's mother. Would you happen to know anything about the damage to Don's bicycle, Chase?"

The young man knew better than to look toward his mother. That would be useless. He'd tried that before, but she didn't come to his rescue. Besides, his pride wouldn't let him stoop that low. Nonetheless, he was so scared he was shaking. Finally, he said, "It was a axee'dent, Walt. And me and Mike tried to fix it the best we could."

"She was not very happy. What happened, son?"

Chase laid it out for him, leaving out not a single detail. "We musta been goin' ninety miles an hour when we hit. I never touched a brake. No sir, I was still pushin' hard on them pedals, tryin' to go faster."

Walt chuckled. "Damn, I'll bet that hurt."

"Yes, Sir. It hurt like ... a lot. But like Mom always says, 'God has a way ...'"

"He does, indeed. While I sympathize with your pain, you had no business *borrowing* your friend's bicycle. You didn't have his permission, and you damaged it. I admire your attempt to repair it, but the damage appears to be beyond your level of expertise, at least from what I'm told.

"The biggest problem is you didn't come clean in the first place. You should have knocked on the door to ask permission. Lacking that, you should have owned your mistake. Now, your only option is to go over there, knock on the Malone's door, and seek forgiveness. I suggest you put some clothes on, fetch Mike, grow up, and take your medicine."

Chase hung his head in defeat, swallowed hard, and said, "Yes, Sir."

He sheepishly opened the passenger door and slid out of the fancy, black convertible that had somehow lost its luster. Gently shutting the massive hunk of steel, he started to walk toward the back of the vehicle, away from his stepfather, when he heard Walt say, "It didn't close all the way."

Frustrated, Chase stopped, stepped back, re-opened the door, and slammed it closed, never looking back at his nemesis.

Walt watched as he, once again, walked around and behind the Ford. "That's better." He grinned as Chase disappeared into the house.

Walt followed a few seconds later to wash his hands in the kitchen sink. He reached for the bar of Lava Doris kept on the windowsill for especially dirty hands. While scrubbing, he asked his wife, "Where did you put the car keys? I'm gonna back it out and put the top up."

Pointing, she replied, "Oh. I laid them there on the breakfast counter behind you. Thanks for doin' that. I should have left it in the driveway instead of pulling it all the way into the carport. I'm sorry."

"No. It's okay. You did what I was hoping you'd do. It worked out well, I think. Don't you?"

Doris smiled. "Yeah. Probably so. I feel kinda bad for the boys, though."

"Maybe, but it's time they suffer the consequences of their actions." Walt grabbed the keys and headed out the door.

CHASE RETURNED FROM his bedroom wearing jeans and a striped T-shirt. Walt was still outside in the driveway. "Mom, do I hafta go over there?"

"I told you this isn't over, young man. I'm afraid your stepfather's right. Since Mrs. Malone stopped by, it's time to 'take your medicine,' as Walt so eloquently put it."

"You heard him, huh?"

Doris smiled. "I expect half the neighborhood heard him. Your stepfather learned to whisper in a sawmill."

"I didn't know he used to work in a sawmill."

Doris giggled. "It's a euphemism, Chase. Go get Mike and get this over with. You'll feel better when it's done."

Chase shrugged, dropped his head, and let out a deep breath. "Yes, ma'am."

STANDING SIDE-BY-SIDE, the two boys knocked on the door in the carport of the Malone's home. It, too, led into the kitchen, much like Chase's house. Don's mother answered. "Well, hello, boys. To what do I owe the pleasure of your visit?"

The culprits flashed a bewildered glance at one another as a lump formed in Chase's throat when he tried to speak. "I ... We're here to confess." Tears began to well.

"Come inside, and you can tell me all about it." She pushed the door open wide and motioned for them to enter. She led them into the living room, offered them a seat, and invited Don and Don Sr. in as well.

Once seated, Mrs. Malone asked, "Would either of you gentlemen like something to drink?"

Too nervous to swallow and fearing they might embarrass themselves by spilling something, both boys declined.

Mrs. Malone then folded her hands across her lap and asked, "Okay. What was it you wanted to confess?"

For the two in the hot seat, all that was missing was the bright light shining in their eyes. They shared another glance, perhaps for reassurance, before Chase realized he was the one who had to do the talking. *Mike ain't gonna say nothin'. He's too chicken.*

Despite that annoying lump that wouldn't go away, Chase began. "We been drooling over Don's new bike ever since the first time we saw it, and he kept leavin' us in the dust. That thing is *so fast*."

He went on to recite the rest of the story. Mike interjected with his perspective whenever he could, especially the part about him landing on the hood and the sound it made.

Don Jr. fought hard, often putting his hand across his mouth to hold back his laughter because he knew he'd end up extending his grounding.

When Chase wrapped up the tale, he said, "We sure are sorry all this happened. We didn't mean to wreck Don's bike, and we know we shouldn't 'a took it without askin', but we just couldn't resist the temptation, I guess. My mom says it's only right if me and Mike pay for the repairs out of our savin's accounts. We promise we won't do anything *that* stupid ag'in."

A pause of several seconds ensued before Mrs. Malone finally spoke. "That was quite a story. And it was a stupid thing for you boys to do. To that, we will agree." She looked at her husband and asked, "What do you think we should do with these scoundrels, Honey?"

"Well, after hearing this saga, I'd say thirty days in solitary confinement might be appropriate, but that won't pay for the repairs. What do you think, my dear?"

"I tend to agree, but the bicycle doesn't quite make it to the level of *grand theft*, so maybe that's a *bit* harsh. And, they did return it, albeit somewhat damaged." Turning her attention back to the boys, she continued. "I'm going to suggest this. We have a lot of chores around here that need doing. I'd hate for you boys to dip into your savings, so I will keep track of the work you do around here for me. I'll pay you a fair wage, say $.75 an hour, and you work it off throughout the school year. Plus, you keep your promise not to do anything that stupid again. Do we have a deal?"

Simultaneously, the boys exuberantly responded, "Yes, ma'am!"

"All right then. You boys go on home and have a nice evening." Speaking to her son, she said, "Don, you may see your friends on their way."

"Yes, ma'am."

The boys stood, and Chase said, "Thank you, Mrs. Malone. When do you want us to report for duty?"

"I'll call your moms, and we'll chat. Together, we'll try and come up with a schedule that works for everybody."

"Okay. Thanks again."

"You're welcome. Good night."

The boys walked into the carport before Don spoke. "That was the funniest story I've ever heard. I about died trying to keep from laughing."

After briefly chatting about that debacle, Chase asked, "What did you do to get grounded?"

"I don't know. Mom was raggin' me about somethin', and I picked the wrong time to say the wrong thing."

"Really? And she grounded you for a *week*? What'd you say?"

"All I said was, 'What's got you on your high horse?'" His expression changed, eyes widened, arms raised. "She went crazy! Musta been ridin' her cotton pony's all I can figure." Don chuckled.

Excited, Mike asked, "You guys got a pony? I didn't know that. Did you, Chase?"

Don looked at them for a moment in amazement. "Neither of you have a clue what I'm talking about, do you?"

Nothing but blank stares. The meaning of his comment sailed right over their heads. "Oh, my God. Have your parents taught you nothin'? Okay, the next time you're with your mothers, and you have her alone, ask her to tell you about menstruation. I promise you it will be an interesting conversation."

A voice from inside the house rang out. "Don. It's time to come in now. Remember, you're still grounded."

"Yes, ma'am." He turned back to his friends and whispered. "Remember, menstruation. See ya' later." Don rushed inside.

On the walk toward his home, Mike asked, "Do you think Don's mom really has a pony?"

"I don't think so, but I'm not sure."

"What do you reckon he was talkin' about with that 'cotton pony' stuff? And what's a men's-station anyway? Is there a woman's-station? Maybe that's where they keep it."

"He didn't say 'men's-station,' he said, 'men's-*tration*.'"

"Oh, there's a 'r' in it then, huh?"

"Yeah. I think so, or it might be a you-me-fism like Mom said."

"A *what*?"

"Never mind."

When they reached Chase's yard, he said, "See ya' tomorrow, Mike."

"Yeah. After *school*, huh?"

"I know. I can't believe our summer is *over*."

"Me neither. We only go half a day, though. How 'bout you?" Mike swatted at a mosquito buzzing near his ear.

"Yeah. Me, too. But I don't know 'bout the bus schedule. I ain't got no idea what time *I'll* git home."

"I hate those darned buses. I'll keep a lookout for ya'. Maybe we'll have time to head back over to the trestle. Hopefully, my dad'll get my bike tire fixed for me."

Chase waved. "Okay. Bye." He turned and headed toward his house.

Though their addresses showed different street names, their homes were accessible without crossing a single road. From his backyard to the left, Chase could see Mike's back door across two neighbors' lawns. If he looked to his right, the patio umbrella behind Don's, three houses down, was in full view. Don's faced the adjoining street.

Mike walked on, mumbling something about ponies and why his friend would have kept that a secret. Chase shook his head as he went inside.

Entering the kitchen, he didn't say a word. He headed toward his room.

He passed behind his mother, who was busy in the kitchen. "Oh, good, you're home. Supper won't be long."

Chase kept walking but murmured, "I'm not hungry."

Doris followed a few seconds later. His door was open, so she tapped on the jamb. "May I come in?"

"I guess." He was sitting on the edge of his bed.

"Are you okay?"

"Yeah."

"What happened? What did Mrs. Malone say?"

"Well, I told her what happened, how sorry we were, and everything. She decided that we should work for her after school this year. She's gonna pay me and Mike seventy-five cents an hour, I think, for whatever she needs done. I guess she's gonna keep track. She said she's gonna call you and Mike's mom to work out some kinda schedule."

"Ohhh." Doris nodded. "That seems mighty fair if you ask me. You should feel pretty lucky she's not pressing charges, you know. What you two did was against the law."

"You really think so? We didn't *steal* the bike. We just *borrowed* it, Mom."

"I'm not sure the law sees it like that, honey. Sorry." Doris patted him on the head and gave him a big hug. "I'm glad this is over and didn't turn out any worse than it did. I'll call you when supper's ready."

As she was about to leave the room, Chase asked, "Mom. What does *men's-tation*, no *men's-tration* mean?"

His mother appeared as though she had seen a ghost. All color left her face. "Where did you hear that word?"

"After Mrs. Malone was done with us, she let Don walk us out to the carport, and I asked him what he did to get grounded. He told us that he smarted off to his mom. He said it wasn't nothin' he hadn't said b'fore, 'cept she musta been ridin' her cotton pony. Me and Mike didn't know what he was talkin' about, so he told us to ask our moms about *men's-tration*. I got no idea what he means. He said if I asked you, it would be an inter'stin' conversation."

Trying to regain her composure, Doris responded. "Don said that, huh?"

"Yeah. He did."

"Well, I guess it's time to fill you in on some of the facts of life. I've got a short book that might shed some light on the subject. Just a minute. I'll be right back."

As she turned to leave, Chase said, "You know I hate to *read*, Mom."

Doris ignored him and returned in less than a minute. "I know you *say* you hate to read, but try this. It has illustrations that explain a lot about male and female anatomy, a woman's reproductive cycle, menstruation, and sexual intercourse—how babies are made. I think you'll find it *very* interesting. When you've finished, we can have a conversation about what you've read. Okay?"

Chase took the book from her hand and, while gazing at the cover, said, "O ... Okay. Thanks, Mom."

"You're welcome. I hope your appetite improves by the time I get supper ready. Enjoy your book." She headed out the door.

DORIS RETURNED TO THE kitchen, where she had laid out several items in preparation for the evening's meal, including the package of meat wrapped in white paper from the supermarket. Walt asked, "How did things go at the Malone's?"

"Sounds like he's pretty beaten up, but all in all, I think it went well. He says Don's mom agreed to let the boys work off the cost of repairs over the school year in exchange for chores around her home." With extra emphasis, she added, "She's going to pay them seventy-five cents an hour."

Walt chuckled. "Ha! That's an awful lot. She probably doesn't want to put up with them any longer than she has to."

With a glass of tea at her lips, Doris raised it as a toast and said, "There's probably a lot of truth in those words."

"What's he doin' now? Is he still in his room?"

"Yeah. Lickin' his wounds, I expect."

# Chapter 6
# The Facts of Life

Chase began reading the book his mother had given him. He was intrigued by the title, *An Illustrated Guide to the Facts of Life*, but was disappointed with the lack of clear and specific images of male or female body parts. He was hoping for photographs in living color. All he got were cross-sectional drawings focusing mainly on internal organs. There was one depicting the penis, scrotum, and testes as a unit[1], but as shown, it failed to resemble anything like what he saw when he looked down at himself. He was confused.

The words and drawings, especially of the female organs, made no sense to him at all.

Chase thumbed through the book repeatedly, looking for a photograph he could understand. *How stupid? I thought this was gonna teach me somethin'.* He slammed it closed.

Staring at the cover, he decided to open it again and force himself to read the first few pages. His eyes found letters assembled in ways he'd never seen before. If they were actually *words*, they were undoubtedly ones that were new to him. His attempt to sound them out phonetically became a cacophony of confusion in his brain. He would later discover that only a few of his attempts were correct, and reading was challenging. *P-e-n-i-s. Pĕnis? Is that what the priest says after confession? Like, "Your pĕnis will be, say two Our Fathers and three Hail*

*Marys, and yer sins'll be forgiven."* Why would he say such a thing? I wonder what he says to girls.

*S-c-r-o-t-u-m. Scrŏtum? What the hell is a scrŏtum? Who came up with a word like that? And Testĕs? Who said anything about tests? They misspell that? Maybe it's a misprint. Maybe they're gonna give us more than one test on this stuff, but they added an 'e' where it shouldn't be. I hate takin' tests. Maybe they should'a took one b'fore they wrote this stupid book.*

*V-a-g-i-n-a. Kinda looks like Virginia. Va-gĭn-a? That doesn't sound right. Maybe it's pronounced Vageena, Like Gina next door?* He looked out his bedroom window. *Maybe that's how she got her name.* He giggled. *To think, bein' named after some girly part. She sure is purdy, though. Who knows what those other things are?*

He glanced back at his book and rubbed his chin. *C-e-r-v-i-x? Like curvy, maybe? I bet they misspelled that, too. They prob'ly meant crucifix. Cause, looking at the drawin',* he held out his arms, mimicking the fallopian tubes. In his mind, he saw Christ hanging on the cross. *The whole thing, the way it's showed, sure looks like one to me. I wonder if this could be a religious thing. Maybe girls get one of those at Confirmation. That's prob'ly why everybody makes such a big deal outta that ceremony. All gussied up in those fancy white dresses and everything.*

*Come to think of it. I'm pretty sure I remember hearin' the nuns talk about those Fallopian people in Catechism class. It's gotta be a religious thing.*

His mother's voice broke his train of thought. "Supper's ready. Wash your hands and come to the table, please."

"Okay" rang out from various rooms around the house.

Frustrated and confused, Chase closed the book once again. *This damned thing ain't answerin' nothin'. I need to git Mom alone to ask her some questions. She's gonna hafta help me out.*

AT DINNER, DORIS BEGAN by saying the usual prayer before the meal, and they all joined in with, "Amen," quickly followed by the sign of the cross.

Walt always began the distribution of food. He would start with the meat, which Mom would always set near his usual seat at the table. On this day, it was cube steak, battered and fried, simmered in gravy until it was quite done. He would choose a piece, put it onto his plate, and pass the platter to Chase, who sat to his left. From there, it would go to Walt's eldest daughter and then to her brother, next in line. It would then skip the youngest child, another daughter, to Mom, who would dip food on the toddler's plate and finally her own.

Today's fare included mashed potatoes, green beans, and yeast rolls with plenty of butter. Chase was *very* happy. He was okay with the cube steak, even though it was always a little chewy for his taste, but he liked Mom's gravy. While not big on potatoes, and he could take or leave the green beans, he could eat his weight in yeast rolls. And if the butter ran out, gravy would do *just* fine. His questions could wait until after supper or until he could get Mom off by herself.

By the time dinner concluded, all the yeast rolls were gone. Chase had used the last one to sop up every last drop of gravy left on his plate. It looked like it had been run through a commercial dishwasher, a luxury not found in *their* home. Doris smiled. "You were hungry."

Walt noticed. "Mrs. Malone musta had ya' pretty nervous. Worked up an appetite?"

Chase shrugged. "I guess. But she was pretty nice about it, really."

Doris beamed. "I am so glad to hear you say that, Chase."

"Well, it's true, Mom. Like you said, 'It coulda been a lot worse.'"

"Still, hearing you say that makes me very happy. Now, everyone, carry your plates to the kitchen, and *I'll* wash the dishes tonight. Y'all start getting ready for bed, and that means baths. You've got school in the morning."

Chase jumped up, grabbed his plate, and said, "I get the tub first." He hurried to the kitchen.

His sister rolled her eyes and said, "I *hate* him."

Doris flashed. "You do not. He thinks about things like that a little quicker than you, that's all. You'll catch on soon enough."

Chase set his plate and silverware next to the sink and headed to the bathroom.

AFTER SEVERAL MINUTES, he heard a knock on the bathroom door. "Hurry up, and don't forget to rinse the tub before you finish. It's my turn, and I don't want to bathe with your nasty bathtub ring. You're so disgusting."

"I'm already out of the tub. You can come on in and start running your water if you want."

"Okay." She opened the door to find her brother wrapped in his towel, parting his hair, and the tub wearing the distinctive soap scum. Pointing, she said, "I told you to rinse this before you finished."

Turning toward her, gesturing forcefully, throwing his arms to his sides, he said, "I'm just tryin' to save you some time—tryin' to be helpful. It seems the least you could do would be to splash some water on the sides and rinse the darned tub. I didn't say I was *finished* anyway."

As she leaned over to turn on the water, his sister said, "I *hate* you."

Looking at himself in the mirror as he combed his hair, Chase mocked her. Mimicking her facial expression, he silently mouthed her words, "I *hate* you," and finished with a little dance. He giggled, put his comb in the medicine cabinet, gathered his clothes, and left the room for his, proud he'd conned sister into rinsing the tub.

She slammed the door behind him.

STEPPING INTO HIS PAJAMA bottoms, Chase heard his mother knock. "May I come in?"

Frantically, he replied. "Just a minute." A few seconds later, "Okay, Mom. The coast is clear."

Cautiously, Doris opened the door and peeked her head around before entering. "Are you okay? What's going on?"

Chase blushed. "When you knocked, I only had one leg in my pajama bottoms. That's all."

Doris chuckled and sat beside him on the bed. "Honey. I've seen you naked a million times. I changed your diapers and gave you baths, remember?" Smiling, she ran her fingers through his hair and continued. "No. I don't suppose you do, now that I think about it. You were mighty young."

"I know you did, Mom, but things are different now." He pointed toward his groin and whispered. "Hairs are startin' to grow down there. Is that normal?"

"Ohhhh. I hate to tell you this, but that's just the beginning of many changes your body's about to experience."

"What does *that* mean?"

"Did you read the book I gave you?"

"Some of it. I expected more pictures. I tried readin', but they're usin' words I ain't never seen b'fore. I don't know how to pronounce 'em or what they mean, so I could read the whole thing, and it still won't teach me nothin'. There ain't a single picture of what a full-grown man or a woman's body looks like. How am I supposed to know what to expect?"

"I understand your concerns about the words. Sounds like this might be harder than I had hoped. Maybe we'll have to read through it together. As to what a man or woman's body looks like, God made a basic pattern, but each one is a little different. I guess that's what makes life so interesting. But there's plenty of time to figure that out in your future."

# Chapter 7
# Raptors and Rum

Chase smiled when he saw Mike straddling his bicycle, waiting for him as he stepped off the school bus.

Mike nodded. "What's with all the books?"

Chase smirked. "I *know*, and this is only *four* of 'em. I figured it's all I could carry on the bus. I wanted Mom to see the kinda hell she's puttin' me through sendin' me to that damned Catholic school."

"Yeah! If you went to *my* school, we'd be at the trestle by now."

Chase didn't stop to chat. He was in a hurry to drop off his armload at home. He started walking when Mike asked, "You're not gonna wait for your sister?"

"She was sittin' with a friend toward the back. She'll prob'ly walk with her. C'mon."

Chase walked while Mike rolled along beside him atop his seat, pushing himself with one foot on the ground until his friend responded. "These things are heavy. I'm supposed to put covers on 'em tonight. We may not have time to go all the way to the trestle, Mike."

"Ah, *man*. We can at least make it to the fort then, huh?"

"Yeah. Fer sure. Ya' got any Coke or 7-Up we can mix with our stash?"

"I've got an idea. Mom bought some Coke at the grocery. When we get up here to the corner, I'll ride to my house, pretend I'm real thirsty, and see if I can talk her into lettin' me have of one to take with me."

"Cool. See if you can bring a glass with some ice, too. Okay?"

"Oh, yeah. Even better. This is gonna be swell."

Suddenly, a voice rang out behind them, "Chase. Wait for me."

"It's your sister."

Chase rolled his eyes. "Duh!"

AT THE CORNER, MIKE took off like a jet. He burst through the door with sweat running down his face. He rode hard all the way, sliding his back tire as he came to a stop in the carport. "Mom. An ice-cold Coke sure sounds good on this hot day after school. Can I have one, please?"

Sitting in the living room watching her favorite soap opera, Mrs. Bifano replied, "I suppose so. Don't make a mess in my kitchen."

"Okay. I'll be careful." Mike opened the freezer to remove the ice tray. He loved lifting the handle and seeing the cubes pop loose. He got a kick out of it whenever he got a chance to do it by himself.

He filled a tall outdoor aluminum *glass* with ice and yelled, "What do you want me to do with the leftovers?"

She smiled at her son's choice of words. "There's a container in the freezer that holds *leftovers*. You probably should have looked there before you emptied a new tray, but that's for another time. Dump them in there, refill the tray, and slide it back where it came from. But be careful you don't spill it as you slide it back in place."

Mrs. B shook her head and went back to watching her TV.

Mike did as instructed and only spilled a little as he awkwardly replaced it. It was when he poured the Coca-Cola over the frozen cubes that things got messy. "Oh, no. Oh, no!"

"What's wrong?"

Mike covered the glass with his hand, but it didn't help. Foam was going everywhere. He tried slurping the spillover, but he couldn't keep up.

It only took an instant for his mother to reach the kitchen. She couldn't hide her amusement. "Do you think you might have poured it a little too fast? Here, let me help." She quickly grabbed the dish rag and began wiping the overflow.

She rinsed, wrung, wiped, and repeated until the calamity was resolved. "There. That wasn't so bad. Now, let me show you a trick." She tipped the cup and gently poured the remainder of the bottle's contents near the rim. "This way, it doesn't foam as much."

WITH HIS ARMS FULL of books, Chase let his sister open the door for him but didn't bother to thank her. When Doris saw her daughter pass by her in the living room, she said, "That's quite a departure from what I'm used to seeing. What's up?"

On her way to her room, Chase's sister replied, "Nothing. Mister Stupid had his hands full and didn't even thank me for opening the door for him. He's not very nice, Mom."

"Chase?"

He dropped his books on the dining table. "I have no idea why she's mad. She would have had to turn the knob if I hadn't been there. What's the big deal? I had my hands full."

"You could have at least thanked your sister."

"Yeah. And you could have slowed down so I didn't have to run to catch up. I hollered at you, but you ignored me."

"I didn't *ignore* you. These books are heavy. I was in a hurry to set them down."

He turned his attention to his mother. "Just look at what yer puttin' me through, Mom. That place is like a torture chamber.

"We don't have no Coke or 7-Up or nothin' like that, do we? No soda pop, right?"

"Son, we've got to work on your grammar, but no. You know I don't buy that kinda stuff. It's carbonated. I don't think it's good for our bodies, and it's too expensive anyway. I do have Kool-Aid."

"Got some already made?"

"I think so. Look in the fridge and see."

Sister, realizing her case had already been dismissed, slipped off to her room—unnoticed.

Chase walked over and opened the refrigerator door. "I don't see any, Mom."

"You don't see the pitcher of Kool-Aid on the shelf next to the milk?"

"No."

Exasperated, Doris exhaled loudly and got up from the sofa. "If that pitcher's in there, I'm gonna bust you, boy."

When she walked by the pile of books on the table, she asked, "Why did you bring these home? Do you have homework already?"

"No. I'm hopin' you'll help me make covers for 'em tonight. And I wanted you to see what I have to go through at that stupid school."

"It's not a 'stupid school.' It's what makes you so smart."

"Are you makin' fun of me, Mom?"

"No! What would make you say that?" Doris walked toward him in the kitchen. "You *are* smart. But you hold the refrigerator door open too long. You know what I've told you about that."

When she took hold of the handle, she noticed the empty pitcher sitting upside down in the dish rack beside the sink, right where she had placed it.

She closed the fridge door. "I'm so sorry, Chase." She pointed toward the sink. "I'll make some while you're changing clothes. Okay? Forgive me?" She brushed her fingers through his hair.

He reached his arms around her waist and hugged her. "It's okay, Mom. Thanks."

In a flash, Chase returned wearing the same jeans and T-shirt he had worn the day before. Doris was still stirring the pitcher.

"Is it okay if I take a glass of Kool-Aid with me to the fort?"

"I guess, if you put it in something unbreakable. You don't need to be taking anything made of *glass* outside."

Chase saw Mike ride up, so he hurried to prepare his drink. He checked the ice bin. *Only three cubes. I don't have time to open a new tray. Three's enough, I guess.*

He poured the Kool-Aid over the ice, grabbed the metal substitute for a glass, and yelled, "Bye, Mom." He closed the door and didn't wait for an answer.

They would ride their bikes half a block from his house to the intersecting road on which Don's house was located. At the corner, the subdivision ended, and the woods began. That's where they would leave their wheeled transportation, ford one leg of the drainage ditch, and enter the woods toward their destination on foot.

With drinks in their hands, crossing the cavernous divide became more of a challenge than usual. Both legs of the ditch were deeper than the boys were tall, and approximately fifteen or twenty feet across. Chase had never seen them when water wasn't flowing, and in the late summer, the vegetation was thick.

Chase held out his cup to Mike. "Here. Hold this for me while I roll up my jeans. Mom'll kill me if I get 'em wet. I've only wore 'em once." He shook his head. "No, this'll be twice, I guess."

Mike held his drink and sneaked a sip. "Eeewww! This is putrid—tastes like Kool-Aid."

Chase grabbed it back from his friend. "Because it *is* Kool-Aid, which I happen to like if you must know."

"I thought you wanted Coke or 7-Up."

"That's what I asked *you* to get." Chase dropped his head and headed for the ditch. "I knew *we* didn't have any. My mom *never* buys that kind of stuff. I only get a Coke if we go to a restaurant and Mom lets us *splurge*."

As he stepped down close to the water, Chase pointed to a stick lying near Mike's foot. It was about as long as his arm. "Hand me that, would ya'?"

"What for?"

"There's a big ol' snake right over there," he nodded in its direction, "and I wanna shoo it away."

"*Bull-shit*! I'm outta here."

"Oh, stop it, *pansy*. He ain't gonna hurt ya'. Just gimme the dad-gum stick."

Mike took a deep breath of courage and did as he was told. When Chase poked the serpent, trying to encourage it to swim on downstream, it chose instead to rise up like a cobra and open its mouth *wide*, ready to attack.

Chase reacted and said, "Whoa there, big'n. What's got *you* so riled?"

He had a healthy respect for snakes, spent time studying them, knew the four poisonous varieties found in Florida, what they looked like, and the shape of their heads. He knew this was *not* one of them.

Mike, on the other hand, responded differently.

From his peripheral vision, Chase saw hands, feet, arms, legs, ice, Coke, and even a cup flying in every direction. His friend was halfway up the bank in the blink of an eye.

Choking back laughter, but without taking his eyes off the reptile, Chase calmly said, "I can't believe you spilled the damned Coke."

"What the hell's the matter with you? That's pro'lly a cottonmouth standing up like that?"

"Mike. Did you see the inside of her mouth? It was black. It woulda been white inside if'n it was a water moccasin. She ain't gonna hurt nobody. She is mighty big around, though, prob'ly gonna have babies soon. Most likely why she's in such a bad mood I reckon."

Chase urged her to move on with his stick, and she finally acquiesced. "See? Now, find yer cup, and let's git on to the fort. Pansy."

"I ain't no *pansy*. I was just *startled*, that's all."

"Uh, huh."

UPON REACHING THEIR makeshift hideout, Chase led the way and ducked through the entrance opening. Mike followed right behind. It was cooler inside, and darker, but there was enough light for them to read the labels on the liquor bottles.

Mike watched Chase twist his cup into the sandy soil, so it sat steady on the ground. Mike started to copy his actions when his friend stopped him. "No, wait. Give me your cup."

"What for?"

Chase reached for his glass. "I'll pour some of my Kool-Aid into yours. It'll be easier to scrunch your glass into the ground with somethin' in it." Pointing to the bottles along the wall, "You spilled yer Coke, so yer gonna need somethin' to mix with that shit. Right?"

"I guess, if you say so. I hate Kool-Aid."

Chase began pouring. "Well, ya shoulda been more careful then, huh?" He handed him back the cup. "This should work better. Whatcha wanna try today? Whatcha s'pose goes good with Kool-Aid?"

"Are you kiddin'? Nothin' *I* know of."

Suddenly, a giant flying bug flew in through a window. Mike jumped to his knees and swatted aimlessly. "What *is* that thing, a hornet?"

Motioning toward his right knee dangerously close to his drink, Chase said, "I don't know, but you better be careful, or yer gonna be left with an empty cup ... *ag'in*! And I'm sure that *bug* didn't fly through the window for the sole purpose of stingin' one of us. Sit still and stop actin' like a girl, afraid of her own shadow."

"I don't like *bugs*, that's all—especially big ones that fly, like *him*." Mike pointed at it and shivered.

"When did you turn into such a pussy?"

Anger flashed on Mike's face. He shoved his friend hard with both hands. "I ain't no *pussy* neither!"

"Okay." Chase straightened his shirt. "That's better. What do you think might taste good with Kool-Aid?"

Mike took a deep breath. He looked toward the liquor bottles and said, "What all do we have again?"

Chase started reading them off in order as they were lined up along the wall. When he got to a particular brand of rum, Mike said, "Rum? Ain't that what the pirates used to drink back when they sailed these parts?"

Chuckling, Chase responded, "Aye, Matey. That's what I've heard."

"Well, they pro'lly didn't have any Coke back then, so maybe they mixed it with fruit juices, huh? Kool-Aid kinda tastes like fruit juice, sort of. Right? Maybe we should try that."

Chase nodded. "Yeah. That *kinda* makes sense."

He grabbed the bottle of rum, opened it, and sniffed its contents, only to quickly pull his head away. "Wow! This stuff is strong. I better pour just a little bit into our glasses to see how it's gonna taste. Okay?"

He poured not more than a teaspoon of the liquid into each cup. They swished it around to ensure it was well mixed and took a sip. They held it in their mouths for a moment before swallowing, then looked at each other with puzzled expressions.

Mike broke the silence. "Did you taste any difference?"

"No. Not much. I'd better add some more."

Before they knew it, the boys found themselves wandering around the woods, talking about anything and everything, including how good that Kool-Aid tasted. They lost track of time—and where they were.

THE SUN HAD SET ON their way back, which made finding their way all the more challenging. Luckily, their path led them past their fort in the fading light, and Mike said, "Hey, we should get our cups."

Chase reached in and grabbed them without paying much attention. He didn't notice they were covered in ants.

Before handing Mike his, he felt the insects biting him, dropped both, and rubbed his hands together to remove the pesky critters. "Ah, *man*. Ants must love rum and Kool-Aid. They're all over our glasses."

They did their best to rid the containers of the invaders by rolling them on the ground and wiping them with nearby weeds. They scooped stragglers out of the interior with their fingers. When they neared their bikes, they rinsed the cups in the ditch as a finishing touch.

Chase felt unusually tired and a little unsteady as he mounted his bicycle, and they parted company. *This is weird. We didn't walk <u>that far</u>.*

Closing the door behind him, he heard his mother's voice from the dining table, "I was wondering if you were going to show up for supper. *We're* nearly finished. Did you get lost or something?"

He dropped his cup in the kitchen sink on his way to where the family was gathered. "I'm sorry, Mom, but yeah. Kinda."

He was in no hurry to leave the shadow of the kitchen since he hadn't taken the time to roll up his jeans when he crossed the ditch coming home. He knew stepping into the lighted dining area would not be met with kindness.

His mother's nostrils flared, and her eyes grew large. She motioned toward the door from whence he came. Through clenched teeth, she said, "Get out of those clothes. I don't want them in my hamper, so take them off in the utility room. Make sure there's nothing in the pockets. Then, go wash your hands and face, put your pajamas on for the time being, and get your ass back in here. I can't wait to hear *this* one."

Chase started to say something, but she interrupted, motioning him away. "Not another word."

When he returned to take his seat, Doris glared at him. Sensing the tension, Walt held the plate of meatloaf for Chase to select one of the remaining slices.

His mother began. "You know the rules. Be home *before* dark. What happened? And how did you get so dirty on a school night?"

"Mike and I were explorin' a part of the woods we ain't ever been b'fore, and we got kinda lost."

"Do you expect me to believe that? I can't imagine there's a part of those woods you haven't been."

With his hands to the side, about shoulder high, palms up, he replied, "Okay. We weren't exactly *lost*."

"That's what I thought."

"I mean, we *kinda* knew where we was. It's just that we was a lot further from where we *thought* we was, and it took us a lot longer for us to get back to where we was *sure* we was, and then to git home, it took *forever*. That's all." Chase tilted his head. "I'm sorry, Mom."

"Well, how'd you get so filthy ... and wet?"

"We was scared."

"Scared? What for? Because of the dark?"

"Kinda, I guess. We knew we was gonna be in trouble 'cause it was *already* dark. We was hurryin' as fast as we could. I didn't think about rollin' my jeans up when we crossed the ditch. Water splashed up everywhere."

His sister snickered. Walt had to turn his head to hide the smile on his face. Little brother giggled.

Doris fumed and slammed her hand on the table. "Stop it! All of you. This *isn't* funny.

"Chase, what would we do if you *did* get lost in those woods in the dark? What if a bear or a panther got hold of you? Or what if a snake bit you?"

Chase eagerly nodded. "That's why you should buy me that huntin' knife I've been askin' for. That way, I could wrestle 'em to the ground and kill 'em or at least have a fightin' chance, Mom."

Doris slapped her hand across her forehead and put both elbows on the table. Looking down, she said, "Dear God, give me strength." After a pause, she uttered, "Eat your supper, Chase."

No one dared speak, but serving dishes containing the remainder of room-temperature food started appearing in front of Chase. Walt handed him the mashed potatoes. His sister placed the spinach bowl on the table beside him and offered another with gravy, perhaps as a peace offering. When he took it from her, he noticed a skin had formed on the surface. It made a chill run down his spine. He shivered, set it aside, and said, "No, thanks."

Seeing his reaction, Doris said, "Oh, for Christ's sake. There's good gravy under that skin. It does that when it sits for a while. And that's what you get for being late like this. It's your own damned fault. Use the spoon, push back the skin, and get to the good gravy. You'll be fine."

"It's okay, Mom. I'm not very hungry tonight anyway."

Chase dipped some spinach onto his plate, along with a small portion of mashed potatoes. "I like potatoes with just salt and pepper, sometimes too, Mom. I don't need gravy *every* time, you know."

"Yeah. I can tell by the enormous *portions* you've dipped onto your plate. Why are you not hungry? After all the exercise you got in the woods, I'd think you'd be starving."

"I guess it's because I'm nervous and in a hurry. Remember, I was hopin' we could put covers on my books."

"I'm afraid you already blew that opportunity. It's too late for that. You still have to finish eating, and since you got so dirty, you *must* take a bath. I did the dishes last night, and I'm not doing them two nights in a row. You and your sister are on this evening. Bring your books back home tomorrow, and we'll put covers on them then—*before* you go to the woods. How's that?"

"Aww, Mom. Yer *killin'* me. I hate school."

"Your bad decisions make things so difficult for you, Chase. I wish you could see that."

Recognizing the futility of further discussion, Chase shook his head and forced down a few bites of the food he found repulsive since it was cold and without gravy. The queeziness of his stomach from his earlier shenanigans didn't make it any easier.

SEEING HER BROTHER struggle to finish the last few bites, his sister headed to the kitchen. She ran soap and hot water into the dishpan, wetted the rag draped across the faucet, and wiped the counter next to the drain rack beside the sink. By the time she cleaned the stove, Chase stood beside her with his plate. He whispered, "Thanks."

She handed him the dishrag, said, "You're welcome," and headed to the dining table to gather the remaining dishes.

They alternated duties, and it was his turn to wash and rinse the dishes tonight. Sister was to wipe the table, counters, and stove, dry and stack the plates for *Mom* to eventually put away. A cost-saving strategy at this stage of their young lives—reaching those high shelves can be difficult for short people.

Everyone was responsible for bringing their plate to the kitchen and scraping uneaten food into the trash. Mom would take care of any leftovers she wanted to save. She left the rest to the children until she came in to inspect the room and put away the remaining items.

Finishing first, Chase ran, with his hands still wet, to get his bath before his sister could hang up the dish towel.

She screamed silently in exasperation, knowing if she was going to bathe, she'd have to deal with his nasty bathtub ring. But most of all, despite being the brother she so admired, Chase seemed to care nothing about her. *Why is he so mean to me?*

WHEN THEY ENTERED THE house on Wednesday, the first full day of school, Chase was carrying the same four books he had the day before. "Hi, guys. You just getting home? What took you so long? It's almost 4:30."

"I *know*! This is *terrible*, Mom. I hafta ride the *second* bus *ag'in*! I *hate* goin' to that stupid school." With tears in his eyes, he dropped his books on the dining table. His sister walked past them almost unnoticed.

"Why do ya' make us *go* to that Catholic school, Mom?"

Doris got up from the sofa and walked toward her son. "I am sorry about the bus. I guess it's because of where we live. I can't control where the diocese draws their routes, Chase. That's out of my control. I send you to that school because we're Catholic, *and* it's where you'll get the best education. It's where you'll learn the things that will help you achieve success in life."

"If it doesn't *kill* me first."

"It's not going to *kill* you. Your sister doesn't seem to mind. I don't hear *her* complaining." Pointing, his mother continued, "See? She's already gone to her room. Did Mike meet you at the bus stop today?"

"*Nobody* was there. Mike prob'ly gave up. And I'm sure she hates it, too. She's just too afraid to say anything."

Ignoring her son's comment about his sister, she said, "Mike's probably doing homework. Do *you* have any?"

"I *did* have, but I had *plenty* of time to get it all done waitin' on that *stupid* bus. We had to sit in a classroom. They called it a study hall. Whoever hearda that?" He lifted the corner of one of his books on the table. "We need to put covers on these. Remember?"

"I'll help with that. If you'll go change clothes, we can work on these whenever you're ready. Okay?"

"Okay, Mom." Chase headed toward his room.

As he walked away, Doris said, "By the way, Mrs. Malone called. She said Don's grounding concludes tonight, so he's free again tomorrow, but she wants you and Mike to work a few hours this weekend. She'd like you boys to report for duty at 9 AM sharp on Saturday. I thought you'd like to know."

Chase stopped but didn't turn around. He hesitated and considered throwing a tantrum but decided against it, rushing to his room instead. Once inside, he closed the door and fell onto the bed. All efforts to stifle his emotions failed. He buried his head in the pillow and cried.

After several minutes of sobbing and feeling sorry for himself, he got up—mostly because he was about to drown in his facial secretions. His pillow was a mess.

The handkerchief he always carried came in handy. He used it to dry his eyes and blow his nose. It quickly found its way into the hamper.

He removed his school uniform, the white, short-sleeved, button-front, collared shirt and khaki pants. He hung the trousers on a hook mounted inside the closet door. The shirt went into the hamper. He knew wearing the same one to school two days in a row was a definite no-no. *Mom'll never let that fly.*

He put on a pair of shorts and a clean T, splashed water on his face, and went to find his mother, who, he soon learned, had already cut apart four grocery bags in preparation for their project.

Standing at the dining table, she could see by his swollen, red eyes that he'd been crying, "Poor baby." She stepped toward him and reached for a hug.

Chase resisted at first but quickly relented, and they embraced. He loved the warmth of his mother's softness. He broke down again. "I hate school, Mom. I have to get up way early to catch that bus. It runs before all my friends' buses, and then I get home later 'n anybody."

"I know, honey. I'm so sorry for that."

"It's just like at the other house."

"Yeah. I was hoping by moving, that would change. I was wrong. I'm sorry." Doris continued to hold him, and they rocked back and forth until she said, "I wish there was something I could do about it, but there isn't.

"I've found some grocery bags we can use to cover your books. Would you like to work on those now? It won't take very long if we do it together, and you can get it behind you." She kissed the top of his head.

With his arms around her waist and his face nestled in her chest, he answered with a muffled reply. "May as well. Looks like my days are shot for the rest of the year, and now, thanks to Mrs. Malone, so are my weekends. My life is *over*."

Through a painful smile, Doris broke their embrace, brushed the hair out of her son's eyes, and said, "Just remember, it's like I always say, 'This, too, shall pass.'" She stepped beside him, wrapped her arm around his shoulder, and walked him to a chair at the dining table, where they worked as a team to cover the books.

# Chapter 8
# Penance

When the guilt-ridden bike rustlers approached the residence on Saturday morning, Mrs. Malone swung the door open and said, "Good morning, gentlemen." She glanced at the clock in the kitchen. "Two minutes late. Punctuality is one thing most employers find essential in their employees, and it pays off, especially when it comes time for raises and promotions. You should think about that in the future."

Mike tilted his head, cocked his brow, and said, "Punctawhat? I've never heard that word before, Ma'am."

Chase looked at his friend like he'd lost his mind. *Surely, he knows what "punctuality" means.*

Mrs. Malone put her hands, palms together, slightly below her chin, as if she were praying, and said, "Punctuality, Michael, means arriving *precisely* on time, or better yet, perhaps, a few minutes early, so you can familiarize yourself with whatever needs doing and prepare for the day's work. That will ensure the greatest productivity. Employers value that highly and will reward it eagerly." She concluded with a distinct nod.

When Chase heard the word *productivity,* he knew he had to act fast. From the look on Mike's face, Chase could tell his friend was about ready to ask a question, and Chase knew they'd be in for another long dissertation, this time about gross domestic product. He gave Mike the quick, half-headshake indicating, in one simple motion, HALT! STOP! DON'T DO IT! NOPE! WHAT WERE YOU THINKING?

Fortunately, Mike got the message and let it go.

Dressed like June Cleaver, Mrs. Malone clapped her hands and turned abruptly. The hem of her dress expanded as it spun. The boys were mesmerized. "Follow me, gentlemen. We've got work to do." She led them toward the patio.

Mike murmured, "Yes, Ma'am."

Chase asked, "Is Don home?"

"No. He's with his father." She stopped, turned, and scowled, "They're picking up the bike you two scoundrels *demolished*." True though it was, she heard their story, their confession, how sorry they were—albeit a tad late—and that they'd been hurt. She quickly faced forward again to hide the grin trying to occupy her face.

She led the boys outside to the flower beds to give them basic instructions.

As they walked together outside, horror built in Chase's mind. *These things go on forever. We'll never git done pullin' weeds.*

"Okay, boys. I'd like you to pull all the weeds from all these beds. Here's a bucket for each of you. Put the weeds in here, and when it gets full, dump it in the garbage can beside the carport and fill it up again. I'll be out to check on you shortly. Any questions?"

Mike said, "Yes, Ma'am. How do I tell the difference between a weed and a flower?"

"Well, Michael. Flowers are the pretty ones and usually bigger and in bloom. The weeds are the nasty little things trying to grow all around the pretty ones, trying to choke them out." Using the yardstick she grabbed as she exited the patio door, she continued, "Here. Let me show you. These tall flowers are gladiolus. They're colorful—and beautiful—but these little ugly things growing around them are weeds. They need to come out. It's important to grab them near the ground and pull straight up so the root comes out, too. Otherwise, they'll grow right back."

Mrs. Malone pointed out several other weeds before saying, "I see your mothers sent you with gloves. That's good because some weeds have thorns. You should wear them. Okay? Do you have a good idea of what needs to be done?"

They both nodded, and Chase said, "Yes, Ma'am."

"Alright, then. I'll go inside and make some fresh lemonade. You'll need something cold to drink in a little while. It's going to be hot today, so I'll keep you both hydrated." She headed toward the house.

Armed with their buckets and a basic understanding of the task at hand, the young arborists began.

They started in the middle of the flower bed, where Mrs. Malone began her demonstration. They were on their knees, working in opposite directions, and they quickly got the hang of it.

It wasn't long before Mike asked, "You reckon she's gonna want us to pull these little-bitty ones out, too?"

His friend replied, "I s'pect so. If we don't, they'll be big'ns by next week."

They had finished the first bed and moved to another along the side of the house where they could see the street. After a few minutes, they saw Don and his dad arrive home with the newly repaired bike protruding from the trunk with the lid tied to the rear bumper with a rope.

Chase could see Don in the passenger seat as the vehicle slowed in front of the house to turn onto the driveway. Their eyes met, and they did what they had seen the coolest of men do—give each other that half nod where you ever so slightly lift your chin, and then, so slowly it's almost imperceptible, return it to its original position.

Chase turned to Mike. "It looks like Don's home."

"Yeah. Did ya' think I didn't see him?"

Chase hoped Don would come out and help pull weeds or at least chat with them, but several minutes passed, and he was nowhere to be found. Chase was disappointed.

Finally, he heard the back door open and close. Then, two voices. Mrs. Malone was talking to her son—until he ran to the water spigot and yelled, "Chase, Mike, C'mon! Mom made some lemonade. She said you should wash your face and hands here with the hose."

The boys jumped up, removed their gloves, and ran to the cool water. Mrs. Malone waited for them on the patio. Standing at the table under the large umbrella, she smiled as the boys bent over to let her son direct the hose to flow over their heads. She chuckled and said, "That's one way to cool off."

After using his hands to wipe the excess water from his face, Chase said, "Yes, Ma'am. I feel a lot better now. It's hot out here. Can't wait to try some a that lemonade."

"Well, come on then. Have a seat. You boys have been workin' hard. Take a few minutes and enjoy yourselves. I'll be inside if you need anything."

As she turned to leave, the boys said in unison, "Thank ya', Ma'am."

Don added, "Thanks, Mom."

When she stepped inside, she took hold of the sliding door, stuck her head out, smiled, and replied, "You're welcome," before pulling it closed.

Chase turned his attention to Don. "How long do you think yer mom is gonna make us pull weeds?"

"I dunno fer sure, but I hope not past lunchtime. If she lets y'all have the afternoon off, maybe we can go to the trestle and catch some crabs. Is my stuff still at the fort?"

Chase replied. "Yeah, but we don't have any bait."

"You don't have any more of that shrimp you had?"

"No, man. It was frozen, and we left it there when you cut yerself. It got real nasty, and it spoilt. The last time me and Mike went there, it was gone."

"Gone?"

Mike chimed in. "Yeah. Package and all." He threw his arms in the air to emphasize. "Disappeared."

Don rubbed his chin. "Hmm. Musta been a possum or somethin'. They like rotten shit like that. They are nasty critters." He turned to Chase. "What did your grandpa use for bait when he used to take you crabbin' off the bridges when you lived down south?"

"Mostly smelly chicken innards and parts left out of the fridge for a day or three. Why?"

"Either of you have chicken for dinner last night or the night before? I think we need to dig through some garbage cans, fellas."

Mike spoke up. "You know, night before last ... I know it wasn't last night, 'cause today's Saturday, and on Friday we always have fish, so it was definitely night before last ..."

Don interrupted. "Okay, good. I'm glad we got that straightened out. Now, what happened on Thursday, Mike?"

Mike looked startled, as if he had to process *Thursday*. "Oh. Yeah. On Thursday, before dinner, I watched my mom cut up this chicken she got from the butcher. She reached in and pulled the neck, guts, and everything out its *butt*! It was the most disgusting thing I ever saw."

Don laughed. "Were all the *guts* in kind of a bag thingy?"

"Yeah. That didn't make any sense."

Don nodded. "Butchers put some of the guts, the innards that some people *eat* .... Can you believe that? The gizzard, liver, and heart in a bag and throw the rest away. What'd yer mom do with that stuff?"

Mike replied, "Oh, there's no way she kept any of that. I could see from the look on her face she was about to gag."

Don turned to Chase. "Looks like we start with Mike's trash can."

They toasted their plan with a big swig of lemonade.

PRECISELY, AT NOON, Mrs. Malone showed up on the patio with a tray containing pimento cheese sandwiches, a bag of potato chips, three clean glasses, and the pitcher, filled once again with ice-cold lemonade. She hollered, "Come on, boys. It's time for lunch." She set the tray on the table and headed back inside.

Chase and Mike ran to the hose and drenched each other in the cool water. When Don came out to join them, he was carrying a roll of paper towels, and Chase asked, "Where have you been?"

"Mom's had me inside doin' a whole list a chores. She even made me use a tiny brush to scrub in the corners of the bathroom floors on my hands and knees! You'd think *I* was the one who wrecked the bike."

Chase salvaged the near catastrophe with his mouth open and the sandwich entering before snorting and erupting in laughter. Mike wasn't far behind. All three cavorted in side-splitting guffaws until Chase finally said, "That's the funniest thing I've ever heard you say."

Don replied, "It's true. I didn't wreck the damned bike. Why's she punishin' me? I got grounded for a whole week just 'cause she got upset over what I said about her *cotton pony*, but I served my sentence."

Mike shook his head. "That don't seem fair to me, Don."

Don looked him square in the eye. "No, it ain't, Mike. Ain't fair a'tal."

"But she don't *seem* like she'd be that way."

"Oh, looks can be deceiving, Mike. Don't let that June Cleaver look fool you. They may share the same first name, but that's where the similarities end. She'll be the first to slip that knife in your back as soon as you turn around if you're not careful, and she won't even bat an eye."

"I didn't know your mom's name was June. How cool is that? Does she really carry a knife?"

"It's a figure of speech, Mike."

Chase snickered and lifted his glass to take a sip of lemonade.

"Shut up, Chase. I think June's pretty nice. She made us lunch, didn't she?"

Chase threw up his hands. "I didn't say a word. Why ya' mad at me?"

Mike glared at him but said nothing.

Chase returned his stare momentarily before turning to Don, saying, "Jeez! What'd I do?"

Don shrugged, turned to Mike, and said, "I wouldn't advise calling her by her first name." He shook his head. "No. You don't wanna do that."

Chase asked, "Do ya' think yer mom's gonna let us quit when we're done eatin'?"

"I dunno, but I wouldn't ask her if I was you. I think it's best if'n ya' just acted like y'all was plannin' on goin' back to pullin' weeds. If she thinks that *you* think yer done, she'll make ya' work longer. I know my mother. She's evil like that."

In unison, the younger boys said, "Ooohh."

Mrs. Malone joined them on the patio. "How was your lunch, boys? Did you enjoy the sandwiches? That was a special pimento cheese recipe handed down from my mother."

Mike was the first to respond. "Oh, yes, Ma'am. It was the best I've ever tasted."

Chase followed up, "I agree. I've never even heard of pimentos in anything 'cept olives, but that was really good. Thank you, Ma'am."

"Wonderful. I'm glad you all enjoyed them. They're one of Don's favorites."

Chase pushed his chair back and started to stand. "But I reckon we'd prob'ly otta be gittin' back to work. We been goofin' off for too long already."

Mrs. Malone motioned with her hand for him to stop. "No, Chase. Sit down. I've decided. You fellas have worked hard for three hours this morning, and it's hot. That's enough for today, and, of course, we'll take tomorrow off, too. I don't believe we should work on the Lord's Day. So, I'll see you both again at 9 AM sharp next Saturday. Is that okay?"

Chase responded, "Oh, yes, Ma'am. That's great. We'll see you then. Does that mean Don's free, too?"

She smiled. "Yes. Don's free, too."

The boys leaped for joy and yelled, "Yay!"

"I don't mean to quell your exuberance, but before you leave, ensure everything's nice and tidy around where you've been working. Remember to take your gloves home with you and empty your buckets. Don will show you where to store them in the utility room. Once that's taken care of, you're free to go. Thank you, gentlemen. Have a good rest of your day." Mrs. Malone gathered up their glasses and soiled paper towels—there wasn't a scrap of sandwich or potato chip left behind—and headed back inside.

At the utility room, the boys agreed to walk to Mike's to dig through his trash for bait. Then, they'd meet with their bikes, and they would ford the ditch. Chase was to have his fishing rod and Don the landing net. They would walk to the fort to gather the rest of Don's gear—the cooking pot, his big knife, kitchen matches, and whatever else they might need. Once they had everything, the boys would return to their bikes for the ride to the trestle.

# Chapter 9
# The Crab Feast

When Mike lifted the lid from his family's garbage can, all three boys jerked their heads back as the stench wafted, driven by the breeze of the flies swarming at the disturbance. Their initial shock was punctuated by a stream of expletives that would make any mother weep as Mike abruptly slammed the lid back in place, saying, "That's disgusting." Fortunately, no mothers were apparently within earshot.

Chase broke the tension by saying, "This should be perfect."

Mike replied, "Are you kidding? You're gonna stick yer hands in that can, Chase?"

"Yeah. Whatever's stinkin' that bad'll be perfect bait fer crabs, dummy."

"Well, that makes no sense. If'n crabs'll eat stuff that smells like that, why would I wanna eat a crab?"

Chase shrugged. "Hmmm. Never thought about it like that. Maybe you shouldn't. All I know is they sure taste good. Guess that'll leave more for me and Don."

"You guys are sick."

Chase removed the lid again and tilted the can to start digging. Don held it in place. It didn't take long until Chase identified the smelly culprit, still wrapped in wet, slimy butcher paper.

He looked at Mike. "You see that newspaper in here? It looks pretty clean and dry. Smooth that out on the ground, would ya'? I'm gonna need that."

Mike followed orders, and his brave friend began, fighting the flies, to unwrap his *treasure* on the cleaner, drier paper. Don was trying his best not to gag. Mike was making all sorts of strange noises but finally squeaked out, "I think I'm gonna puke."

Chase found a scrap of discarded wax paper to shield his fingers as he pulled the chicken neck from the gooey, decomposing innards. He laid it by itself on a separate piece of newspaper. "This'll be all we'll need." He pushed everything else back in the can, and Don set it upright. Mike quickly replaced the lid.

Chase rolled the chicken neck tightly in the newspaper and said, "Mike, you got any soap out here? Anythin' to get this smell off me?"

Mike ran into the utility room at the end of the carport—there was no way he was going inside the house. He came out with a handful of powdered laundry detergent. "This is all I could find. Reckon it'll work? It says on the box that it gets odors outta clothes."

Taking it from his friend, Chase said, "I guess it'll have to do." He glanced over and noticed the water spigot. "Ah, man! Yer hose is hooked up to the damn sprinkler."

Mike said, "It don't matter none. Don, you run and grab the whirlygig and hold it on its side so it don't twirl. I'll turn the water on so just a dribble's comin' out, and Chase can wash his hands. Okay?"

"We *could* just unscrew the hose, you know."

"Don, have you met my dad? I'm sure he tightened it with a big ole pair a pliers. We'll never get that thing loose. B'sides, this way'll be a lot faster, and we won't have to put nothin' back."

"Okay. Have it your way." Don lifted the sprinkler and said, "Let 'er rip."

Whoever shut off the valve last made sure there would be no leakage. Mike struggled with all his might to break it loose. When he finally succeeded, it opened a bit farther than he anticipated. "Ooops. Sorry."

He quickly shut it off, but a burst of water shot forth from the sprinkler, blowing much of the powder from Chase's hands.

Chase yelled, "Miiike!"

Don laughed. "Thought you were gonna open it slow."

"I'm *sorry*! It was really tight—had to use both hands. I'll do better this time."

Mike followed through on his promise, and Chase used what powder was left to scrub as hard as he could to remove the stink from his fingers, hands, and forearms.

With his hands still wet, he handed Mike the tightly wrapped chicken neck. "Here. We'll meet you at the ditch. See ya.'"

"Why do I have to carry that nasty thing?"

"Cause I'll be totin' my fishin' pole, and Don's gotta get his landing net, that's why. Have ya' forgotten the plan already? We'll catch up in no time." Chase and Don turned and ran toward their respective homes.

They met Mike at the appointed spot, dropped their bikes, and were at the fort in a flash. Don threw his newspaper bag out the entrance. "We better fill that thing outside; otherwise, it won't fit through the doorway. Mike, you go out there and put stuff in it that Chase hands you, okay?"

"Sure, boss." Mike stepped into the daylight.

Chase knelt at the door and said, "You can start with the bait yer carryin.'" He then handed out the cooking pot, Don's big knife, kitchen matches, and a hammer. That's when Don eyed the bottles of liquor lined against the wall in order of size. The larger bottles were to the left, gradually working down to the pint and half-pint bottles on the right. They were two rows deep. There must have been thirty or more in total.

Having little experience with liquor, Don selected two half-pint bottles. One Canadian Club and another, Peppermint Schnapps, to add to their cache. Handing them to Chase, he said, "We should take along something to drink, don't you think?"

"Sounds like a good idea to me." Chase held on to them as he stepped outside and dropped them in the bag.

The boys left the fort and headed for their bikes. As they were about to mount up, and Don was securing the load on his back, Chase asked, "Should we gather some firewood here and carry it with us?"

Don looked at him like he had two heads. "*Hell* no! Whaddya got, shit fer brains? I'd be the one havin' ta carry it, dumbass. Git on yer bike."

Chase threw his leg over his seat. "You don't have to git all pissy about it. I was just askin'."

"Uh, huh. Try to keep up, would ya'?"

DON, ON HIS NEWLY REPAIRED English racer, was at least a hundred yards ahead of the other two when he noticed a small charcoal grill dumped alongside the road. He stopped to check it out and found its round, wire grate. *This'll come in handy.* He picked it up and dropped it in his bag.

Despite the stop, by the time the others showed up, he had already stashed his bike out of sight in the woods, near where the tracks crossed the road, walked to the trestle, down to the creek's edge, located where they would build their fire and had things unloaded. When they approached, Don said, "Okay. You two need to search for firewood. I'll build a rock ring for it."

Around the trestle, it was easy for Don to find plenty of what he was looking for. He collected enough to configure the outer circumference and three others, somewhat larger, that would serve as the support for the cooking pot in the center. He then gathered twigs and dried grass to use as kindling.

Before long, Chase and Mike had accumulated a sizable pile of sticks and branches. Don got the flame going and slowly added a few more pieces of wood. Once comfortable with how it was burning, he said, "Okay, Chase. Let's see if those crabs like your rotten chicken neck."

Staring into the fire, Chase seemed to have drifted off into a trance—mesmerized.

"Chase!"

He jerked his head up. "Huh?"

"Let's see if those crabs like your rotten chicken neck."

"Oh. Good idea."

"Where *were* you?"

"Whaddya mean? I was right here."

His friends laughed. Don said, "No, you weren't. I'm not sure *where* you were, but it wasn't here."

"Shut up. Lemme git my fishin' pole."

Chase got up and gathered his rod and the bait. He sat down at his favorite spot on the creek bank and opened the newspaper to reveal the stinky, rotting fowl. "Yep. It still smells awful. It should work just fine. Don, I'm gonna need yer knife."

When Don arrived, Chase said, "You'll prob'ly have to cut through the bone. I just need a little piece." He glanced up with a smirk. "Try not to cut yerself this time. Okay?"

Don gave him the evil eye. "Don't git smart with me, dumbass." He set a piece of firewood under the newspaper to support the blade when he pressed down. "Here you go. Is this big enough?"

"That's perfect," replied Chase as he slid it onto his hook and dug his fingers into the sand to rid them of the stink.

He dropped the bait into the water and let it fall near the submerged log where Chase knew crabs liked to hide. Almost immediately, one came out to investigate. "Yep. Check it out, guys. This is gonna work like a charm."

Don ran to get the net. In less than two minutes, they had captured their first blue crab. "Mike, fill the pot with water."

Apparently in shock, Mike said, "What? Me? How? It's yer pot. Why don't you fill it?"

Frustrated, Don handed him the net containing the hostile crab. "If you were any dumber, you'd be a rock. Watch and learn. But don't let him git out!" Don grabbed the pot, marched upstream to the trestle, stepped onto the boulders, and dunked it into the flowing water. He sloshed around the first fill and dumped it to rinse any debris it might have collected on the ride before refilling for the intended purpose—the boiling of their catch.

Chase hollered. "Mike. I need you over here with the net."

"What am I s'posed to do with the one that's already in here?"

"Dump 'im in the pot, fer Christ's sake. Git over here. This'n ain't gonna hold on ferever."

Frantically, Mike darted from place to place. Don was still walking toward the fire carrying the pot. Chase had the second crab hangin' onto the chicken neck—but for how long?

When Mike reached Don, he held the net over the pot and tried to shake the crab free, hoping it would fall into the water. Its legs were tangled in the webbing, seeming to hang on for dear life.

Don said, "Just reach in and grab him from behind. Pull him out and plop him in the pot. Hurry up. Chase's got another one."

"No! He'll pinch me!"

"You're such a pussy. He can't pinch you if you go at him from behind. Trust me, Mike."

Mike reached in, but there was no trust there. He was tentative as he approached. The crab turned and raised his claw in attack mode. Mike jerked his hand back. "I thought you said ..."

"You can't give him that much time, pussy." Don placed the pot on the three rocks over the fire. "Give me the net."

He set the crab on the bank, still inside the webbing, and pressed the rim of the net against the top of his shell. Don maneuvered his hand toward the crustacean's back and lifted him out. He dropped the angry critter into the pot, quickly covering it with the wire grate. They soon realized they'd have to hold it in place with a long stick until they could find another rock heavy enough to weight it down against the efforts of the maniacal crab's escape attempts.

Chase screamed, "Hurry up, Mike!"

His friend rushed over and shoved the net into the water, but the crab saw him coming. He let go of the bait and hightailed it for cover.

"Damn it, Mike. Ya' can't come runnin' up here like some fool thinkin' the crab can't see ya'. They got eyes, you know?"

Mike must have felt awful and tried to defend himself. "You said to hurry, Chase."

"I know. Let's give him a minute or two and see if'n he'll come out and try it ag'in." He pointed down the bank. "Go over there a few feet and lay the net in the water. If he comes back, I'll try to drag him over it. When I do, lift the handle—but not till I tell ya'. Okay?"

Mike nodded. "Got it." He moved downstream about the length of his friend's fishing rod and looked back.

"That's perfect," Chase whispered.

Mike sat cross-legged on the bank and gently placed the net on the creek bottom, holding tight onto the handle.

Don stayed with the persistent crustacean in the warming water. "This guy's doin' his damnedest to get outta here." He laughed. "If his pinchers were any sharper, I swear he'd cut this wire grate in two."

Both boys chuckled, and Chase replied. "Ain't that water boilin' yet? I'da thought he'd be dead by now."

"Naw. It ain't hot enough, I guess."

Chase couldn't resist. "You don't need to just stand over the thing and watch it. Remember what my mom said about that, 'The water'll never boil if ya' keep watchin' it.'"

Mike piped up. "Yeah. My mom talks about 'watched pots' all the time, but I'm not sure what she means. I ain't never seen a pot with a watch on it."

Don and Chase burst out laughing.

"What's so funny?"

When they gathered their composure, Don said, "Nevermind—"

Chase interrupted, saying, "Don, I still don't know what 'men's-tration' means."

"I thought you were gonna ask your mom."

"I did. She gave me a stupid book that had a bunch of words that didn't mean much to me—not a single one about men's-tration. It even had a couple of pictures, well, drawings, really. It had to be a religious book 'cause the drawing of the female parts looked like a crucifix. Somethin' yer s'posed to pray over maybe? It even showed the fallopian tubes. I guess that's where those people traveled to stay safe way back then. I didn't know what that had to do with anything, so I closed the book and said, 'To hell with it.'"

"Well, why didn't you ask yer mom ag'in?"

"When I asked the first time, I could tell she didn't want to talk about it. She couldn't rush outta my room fast enough. When she came back with the book, she handed it to me and left like her pants were on fire."

Mike was as quiet as a church mouse. His eyes were glued to the water.

Don replied, "Ooohh. All right. I'll try to explain it then. Every month, almost like clockwork, women, after they reach puberty, which is what you fellas are going through right now, girls go through it, too." He pushed out his chest, exhaled, stood a little taller, and said, "Yeah. I'm already done with that."

He paused to see if either would ask a question. Neither did, so he continued. "Yeah, except girls start growing boobs and get their period."

Don paused again. Surely, this would stimulate something. Silence. Both boys were transfixed on their tasks in the creek. "Are you listening?"

Chase replied. "Yeah. Boobs and their periods. What's a period?"

"Ahhh. That's where menstruation comes in. You see, their 'period' is the time during which they menstruate—they bleed from their private parts. They have to wear this big, thick band-aid kinda thing between their legs, sometimes for as long as a week before they stop bleeding completely. Now, you can see why women get so cranky and irritable during this time. Right?"

Chase turned his head slowly toward Don. "You're makin' this shit up, ain't ya'? That's the biggest bunch a crap I ever heard. Women bleed fer a week ever month and have to wear a big band-aid between their legs the whole time? Shiiit! They'd bleed to death. And what keeps the thing in place? The glue'd tear their skin to pieces. Don't listen to him, Mike. He's just yankin' our chain."

Don couldn't help but laugh. "I'm tellin' ya' the truth, guys. I'd swear on the Bible if we had one. Every word's the gospel. That big band-aid I was talkin' about, don't use no glue. The brand my mom buys is called Kotex. You ever seen a box of 'em in either of yer homes?"

Chase and Mike looked at each other in amazement, with eyes that had grown huge. Mike said, "I've seen them in our house when mom's bringin' in groceries."

Chase replied. "Me too, in a blue box, I think. Right?"

Mike nodded. "I believe so, but I never knew what they were, and mom's always quick to put them someplace where I never see them again."

Chase appeared dumbfounded and was about to say something when Mike spoke up. "Hey, there's a crab nibblin' on your bait."

"Huh, sure 'nuff. Let him git a good hold on it b'fore I try to drag him over." Chase whispered to the hungry critter, "That's it, grab on real tight, little buddy."

Gently, he lifted his rod tip and moved the bait slowly above the submerged net. When he had him right where he wanted, Chase said softly, "Now, Mike."

They had their second catch safely in the webbing. Mike was excited. He had redeemed himself. Now, could he summon the courage to remove the crab from the net with his bare hands?

Don must have seen his angst because he took pity and helped guide him. "You saw me with the first one. Just do what I did. You got this." He stayed by Mike's side and offered encouragement. "Easy. Yeah, that's it. Way to go."

Mike had the crab firmly in his grip. That's when the realization hit Don. *That fire's goin' mighty good, and we don't have any potholders. How the hell am I gonna lift the wire grate without dumpin' that big ole' rock into the coals?*

"Hold onto that crab, Mike. I gotta find me a couple a sticks I can use to lift that grate."

Excitedly, Mike responded. "You better hurry. This guy's gettin' pretty angry."

"That's why you need to hold on tight."

Don used his chef's knife to hack down two saplings and remove their limbs. He then ran back to where the others were. "These should do."

Mike appeared to be about to panic. His hand was shaking, afraid he would lose his grip on the agitated crustacean. "Thank God! What took you so long? There's plenty of sticks all around here."

"True, but do you see any long enough? I figured I needed green wood, so I cut me some. These shouldn't light up as soon as I git 'em over the flames. That fire's pretty hot, and the rock on top is heavy. You drop that guy into the water when I lift the grate out of the way. Okay?"

Mike nodded. "Okay, but let's hurry."

Don placed his sticks under the grate, which was considerably larger than the pot's circumference. He lifted and moved it to the side, saying, "Okay, Mike. Toss him in."

The first crab had succumbed to the heat and was already turning red. Mike added the second to the cauldron, and Don quickly replaced the grate to prevent his panicky escape attempt.

"Good job, Mike," Don said just before Chase hollered.

"Hurry up, you two. I've got another one, and I need that net in the water."

They replayed the same routine until there were six crabs in the pot. That's when Don said, "That's about all this contraption'll hold, so ease up there, Moby Dick."

With his chicken neck back in the water, Chase jerked his head around and said, "You talkin' to me? We got a system workin' here."

"I know. But catch another'n, and whatcha gonna do with it?" Don pointed at the pot and shifted his weight to one leg. "It dern sure ain't gonna fit in here."

Chase laughed. "Ha! That sounded just like my mom. All you needed was a *dress*."

That remark flew all over Don. He ran toward Chase with a vengeance, saying, "Take that back!"

Before Chase could do anything but drop his fishing rod, Don layed into him with his shoulder, and they crashed into the creek.

When the melee was over, which didn't take long, perhaps the water had served to cool the temperature, Chase said, "I didn't mean nothin' by it. It was a joke ... asshole."

"I know. I didn't like how it sounded, that's all."

They stepped out of the water and made their way near the flames. Before their clothes were completely dry, Don, seeing the escape of a crab was no longer an issue, lifted the grate with those sticks and placed it on the ground beside the fire ring. Gazing into the pot, he said, "How do we know when these are done, Chase?"

His friend looked into the boiling cauldron. "My grandpa told me, once they turn good'n red, they're done. So, I'd say ..." he rubbed his hands together in anticipation, "... they're ready to eat."

The eager boys watched as Don used the sticks he'd cut to lift the heavy cooking pot off its perch above the flames. He set it on the wire grate for stability. It was then Don realized their next problem. *How am I gonna get them crabs outta the hot water? We don't have nothin' but a hammer and my knife.*

He sat there for a minute before an idea came to him. He quickly selected a couple of unused branches and two smaller sticks from their firewood pile. Don placed the branches close enough to support the wire grate and handed the smaller sticks to Chase.

"What're these for?"

"Just take them. That grate is still prob'ly too hot to touch. Yer gonna use them sticks to drag it into the creek to cool when I lift the pot off it. Okay?"

The three boys stared at each other motionless.

Don reiterated, "Okay?"

Chase and Mike, in unison, said, "Why?"

"So, you can touch it without burnin' your fingers. I'm just thinkin' a you, man."

Chase looked at Mike, then to Don. "Why do I wanna touch it with my fingers a'tall?"

"We need to git them crabs outta that pot, and we ain't got nothin' to do it with. So, I come up with this plan. Just do it, would ya'? We don't want 'em ta git all waterlogged sittin' in there till we can stick our hand in it."

Chase laughed again. "They been in water their whole lives, fool."

Mike guffawed. "Ha! Been in water their whole lives. Good one, Chase."

The look Don flashed shut Mike up real quick. "Sorry, Don. That wasn't a bit funny, Chase." Mike turned and acted busy straightening the firewood pile.

While Chase loved to 'poke the bear,' his clothes still hadn't completely dried from the last skirmish. "Alright. What is it you want me to do?"

Don's tone was unmistakable. "Use these sticks in case the grate is still too hot to touch. When I lift the pot, take the grate to the creek and drop it right at the edge. Soon as it's cool enough, put it across these branches here." He pointed. "Once you've done that, I can dump the pot onto the grate. The water'll run through, and the crabs'll stay on top."

Both boys chimed in. "Ooohhh."

Chase added, "Great idea. And I'll try to make the grate nice and level."

Don shook his head. "I'm surrounded by geniuses."

The plan worked like a charm. Soon, six crabs rested on the grate, ranging from extra rare to very well done. Chase was the only one with any experience with cracking open a crab. The only utensils they had at their disposal were the hammer they brought along, Don's chef's knife, and whatever they could fashion from their imagination.

After a long silence, while the boys sat and stared at the steaming mound of red-colored crustaceans, Chase finally jumped up and ran toward the trestle.

Mike hollered, "Where are you going?"

Chase ignored him and appeared to be glancing around at the ground. Don shouted, "What you doin'?"

"Looking for the right rock." He bent down and picked one up. "This'll do. Git over here, you guys. Yer gonna need one a these." He set it in the creek and used his right hand to scrub the flat surface free of accumulated sand and debris.

Don asked, "What for?"

With a mighty grunt, Chase stood up with the rock in his hand. "B'cause this, my friends, is gonna be my *plate*. Ya' see this nice flat side? I can use the hammer to crack open the shell of them there crabs and enjoy my feast." A big grin formed across his face.

Mike climbed to his feet. "Great idea, Chase. You're so smart."

"Oh, puulleeze! I was gonna suggest somethin' like that. He just beat me to it," Don said as he got up, brushed the sand from his pants, and headed for the trestle.

Being the first one ready with a *plate*, Chase nestled his rock in the sand so the flat side was up, level, front, and center, next to the awaiting fare. He located the hammer, selected a crustacean, and readied it for what was to follow. That's when he yelled, "What's the hold-up? I'm starvin.'"

Frustrated, Don replied, "I think you got about the only flat rock over here, but we found a couple that'll work. We're comin', dickwad."

Chase giggled and said, "Okay, but hurry up. These crabs are gittin' cold."

The two rushed over and took up positions on either side of Chase. Once they made their selections, Chase began his instructions. "The first thing we're gonna do is remove the arms with the pinchers." He picked up his crab to demonstrate. "I start with the biggest pincher first 'cause these bottom parts are gonna come in handy. Pull off the whole arm right here at the body." He snapped it off and laid the crab back on his rock.

"Next, I'm gonna remove the smaller part of the pincher itself. Pull it back until you hear it snap, then pull it straight out. There's usually some meat attached to it." Chase demonstrated, stuck the end in his mouth, and removed the meat with his teeth. "Delicious." Holding it up, he said, "Don't throw this away. It works as a great digger-outer to git to those places that's hard to git to." He continued with his demonstration on the legs.

"Now, when ya' use the hammer, ya' can't just waylay the poor guy, or you'll crash the shell into the meat, and ya' don't want that. Ya' gotta keep tappin' a little harder each time until ya' hear the shell crack. Got it? That way, ya' can pry it open and git to the meat without ruinin' it. "It's better that way. And that's when you'll thank me for savin' those little pinchers."

The boys followed Chase's lead, and they feasted ... with only a few mishaps. The boys thought they were in heaven despite the lack of seasonings, drawn butter, or other enhancements.

Mike said, "I think I've got a piece of shell stuck in my throat, and we don't have anything to drink."

It occurred to Don. "Hey, I brought a couple bottles from our stash."

He hurried over to his newspaper bag, where they were hiding. Walking back, he read the labels. "Canadian Club or Peppermint Schnapps, what's your preference, Mike?"

"I have no idea, but I like peppermint. I think I'll try that."

Don handed him the bottle as he passed by on the way to his seat.

"Thanks," Mike said. He opened the bottle and took a swig. "Holy crap. This tastes like cough syrup."

Chase's head snapped toward his friend. *Why would a drink sold in a tavern taste like cough syrup?* "It might make yer throat feel better. Isn't that what cough syrup is supposed to do?"

Mike thought about it for a second. "Maybe you're right." He took another swallow.

Don and Chase watched. "I think it might be helping," Mike said, took another swig, and returned to eating.

"I wonder what this Canadian Club tastes like." Don took a sip, shook his head as if to question the decision, and handed it to Chase.

"That bad, eh?"

After he forced the swallow, Don coughed and said, "No, it's good. A little strong, that's all." Tears formed in the corner of his eyes.

Chase took the bottle from his friend. "Uh, yeah. I can see how strong it must be. It's got ya' cryin' already."

"I ain't cryin'! It burned a little, and I wasn't ready fer it." Don fisted him on the shoulder.

"Ouch!" Chase flinched before taking a sip but was careful to make it a little one. He held it in his mouth until he couldn't stand the burn any longer. He swallowed and was surprised it didn't burn any more than it did as it slid down his throat like his first attempt several days prior at the fort when they all chugged a big gulp together.

Perhaps his brain signaled his salivary glands to flood the invading liquid to extinguish that burning fire. Maybe that helped soften the blow. Whatever it was, he turned to Don and proclaimed, "Hey, that's not bad." He took another sip and offered it back to his friend.

Chase enjoyed the look on Don's face. Being the oldest of the group by more than a year and vastly more physically mature, Don had already ceded more leadership to Chase on this trip than he liked because of his crabbing experience with his grandpa. There was no way he would be outdone when it came to drinking whiskey. "Give me that bottle. It prob'ly just went down the wrong pipe. That's all."

Don took another swig, bigger this time, and followed Chase's lead. He held it in his mouth, swished it around, looked back and forth at both boys, nodded, and hummed, "Mmmm." Finally, he swallowed and finished with, "Ahhhh," followed by another darned cough he couldn't fight off. It was too big for even a *fourteen-year-old boy* to endure without at least one cough. "*Damn it!* It was pretty good, though. You wanna try some, Mike? You've been mighty quiet over there."

Mike didn't say anything. He was still digging in his second crab.

Chase watched him and noticed he was having trouble using the pincher as a tool. He kept dropping it. Holding it between his fingers appeared to have become difficult for him. "Are you okay, Mike?"

"I ... I'm ... fine. I ... uh ... can't feel my fingers ... and my eyes keep moving around. That's all."

The other two looked at each other, and Chase whispered to Don. "Is he drunk?"

Don whispered back, "Dunno, but we better take that peppermint shit away from him. His mom'll kill us."

"That's fer sure." Chase looked back at Mike and asked, "Can I try some a that peppermint stuff you been drinkin'?"

Mike handed it to him and said, "Shhhurrrr. Here you go."

Chase held the bottle up, glanced at Don, pointed, and said, "He already drank nearly half the bottle," before sneaking a taste for himself. His eyes grew big, and he whispered to Don, "It's no wonder. This stuff's pretty good."

Don took a sip and nodded in agreement.

Chase turned his attention back to Mike. "Where's the cap?"

"Huh? I didn't wear a cap."

"No, the lid for this peppermint stuff." Don held up the bottle.

"Oh." Mike looked around him. "It's ... around here somewhere."

That's when Chase knew if it were to be found, he would have to be the one to find it. Fortunately, it was tucked beside the rock Mike used as a plate.

Once located, Chase noticed it was covered with sand. "I better rinse it in the creek b'fore we put it back on the bottle."

Mike objected. "Wha ... why ... would you do that? Ah ... I don't remember shaying ... are we finished?"

Don was quick to answer. "B'cause we gotta be gittin' back soon. That's why. And the way yer actin', I ain't sure you can walk, let alone ride yer bike."

Mike straightened up and looked at Don. "Wha ... are you shaying?"

"I'm saying, I think you've had too much of that cough syrup."

"Nah-uh."

Chase retorted, "Yeah. We think yer drunk." He turned his attention to Don. "We can't let him go home like this. How long you reckon it'll take for this to wear off?"

"No idea, but it's better we get in trouble for bein' late than him walkin' up to his mom in this kinda shape."

Chase grabbed Mike by the arm and said, "Get up. Let's see if you can even stand."

"Let go." Mike jerked his arm away and managed on his own. "See? I'm fine." His attempt to stand wasn't the most graceful, but he was upright.

Chase reached for him. "Let's see you take a few steps."

Mike protested. "I've got this. I told you. 'I'm fine,' and I wasn't kidding."

"Okay, then. Let's see you walk around a little."

"Fine. If it'll make you happy." Mike reluctantly walked up and down the bank and circled around the fire. "Do you mind if I finish my crab now?"

Mike's attempt at walking was a little unsteady, but it seemed to help his situation. Don said, "Yeah, Mike. Finish your crab. We'll leave you alone. Chase and I are gonna check out the pile of bottles on the other side of the trestle and see if we can find any more that ain't broke. Okay?"

"Perfect. That way ... I can eat in peace."

Don grabbed his newspaper bag, and he and Chase headed to the trestle.

THE TWO BOYS WERE IN no hurry as they dug through the pile of broken glass. They wanted to give Mike as much time to recover as possible. As a result, they found dozens more bottles with the seals still intact.

Being careful to avoid cutting themselves, the two boys loaded them into Don's bag and discovered, once again, there were more than he could carry if he were to save room for their utensils.

When they returned to their fishing area, they found Mike had been busy cleaning up the scraps from their meal.

"What'd you do with all the shells? Did ya' eat them, too?" Don asked Mike as he was skittering about. Don couldn't help but laugh at his own joke even though he wouldn't put it past his friend, given his condition earlier.

"No, Don. I didn't eat them. I threw them back into the creek—at different spots downstream. I figured that was best."

Don nodded. "Yeah. S'pect so," before gathering the items to put in his bag that he would carry back to the fort.

Chase picked up his fishing rod and let out about four feet of line. He used the rod to vigorously slam the piece of chicken neck hard onto the creek surface repeatedly, splashing water with every attempt.

Annoyed, Mike yelled, "What in the world are you doing, Chase?"

"Tryin' to git that stinkin' thing off my dern hook. Whaddya think I'm doin'? I don't wanna touch it ag'in. I just washed my hands."

Don spoke up, "Yeah. Don't wanna do that too many times in one day."

Mike's confusion was apparent. "Really? Why not?"

Chase snorted.

Don smiled, shook his head, and mumbled, "Never mind." He filled the cooking pot with water from the creek and doused the fire. "You about ready, Chase?"

Resorting to placing the chicken neck on the sand, Chase held it down with the sole of his shoe and removed the hook. "There. I didn't have to touch it after all." He kicked the stinky hunk of nasty into the creek. He was proud of himself. "Okay, I'm ready. Let's go." He grabbed his rod, secured the hook, and followed the others.

Don had already loaded the newspaper bag onto his back and was heading up the incline to the tracks with Mike right on his tail when Chase noticed the bottle of Peppermint Schnapps lying in the sand. He picked it up.

When he caught up with them at the bikes, he handed the bottle to Don. "Here. Ya' must have missed this when ya' was packin' up."

"Oh. Thanks." Instead of having Chase add it to the awkward load on his back, Don stuffed the half-pint bottle in the rear pocket of his jeans. They headed toward their fort, where they would store the newspaper delivery bag and its contents.

They hurried to get to their respective homes since the sun had set, and dusk was upon them.

Don propped his now-repaired English racer on its kickstand in the carport. The light was on in the kitchen, and he could see his mother's silhouette through the frosted panes of jalousie louvers in the door. She was standing at the stove preparing dinner.

As he passed behind her, he said, "Hi, Mom."

Just before he turned toward his room, she looked up from the frying pan, wearing pearls and an apron covering a bright red, shirt-waisted dress and matching pumps. *"Donald."* Her stern response stopped him in his tracks. "What's that protruding from your hip pocket?"

The End

# Don't miss out!

Visit the website below and you can sign up to receive emails whenever K G Wauthier publishes a new book. There's no charge and no obligation.

https://books2read.com/r/B-A-AFBS-KKXBF

Did you love *Chase And The Spirits of The Trestle*? Then you should read *The Greatest Softball Game*[1] by K G Wauthier!

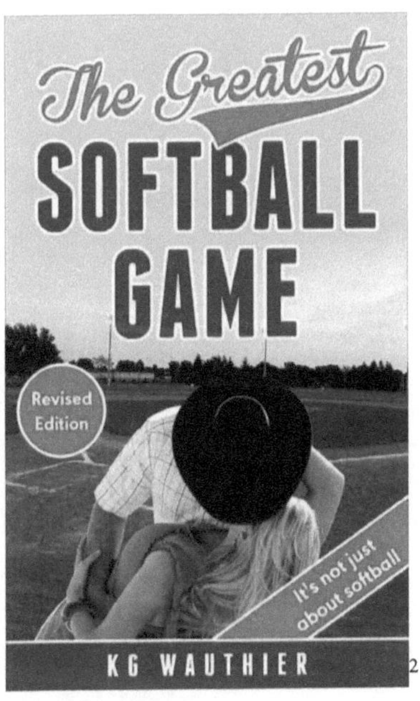


[2]

This is a story about a couple separated by circumstances for 18 years and how they reunited. It is a tragic yet beautiful story for which each paid a large toll. It tells how they met, the trials and tribulations each endured along the way, and the people harmed in the wake of their actions to ultimately get back together.

Despite the lack of two-way communication during the separation, their mutual hunger for one another never died. When their paths once again crossed, it was obvious the flame had not died. The sex was magnificent. This story explores the challenges they faced with a now 20-year-old, head-strong daughter who makes life as difficult

---

1. https://books2read.com/u/mZZGZJ

2. https://books2read.com/u/mZZGZJ

as possible for everyone and how a surprise comes along to help the extended families heal.

Read more at https://books2read.com/greatestgame.

# Also by K G Wauthier

**The Greatest Games Series with Jake & Matti**
The Greatest Softball Game


**Standalone**
Chase And The Spirits of The Trestle


Watch for more at https://books2read.com/greatestgame.

# About the Author

K G Wauthier is a decorated combat veteran who served in Vietnam. He was born in the Midwest but spent his development years growing up in California and Florida, where he gained a wealth of experience.

He met and married the woman of his dreams when he was eighteen, and they have built a relationship that endures to this day. Together, they took on life and the world headlong, continuing to add to his experience.

The Greatest Softball Game is his first book. It's a series of events that could happen to real people, sprinkled with the spice of sexual escapades from his own experiences, that will leave you eager to read about their next adventures.

Be on the lookout for his next book, Chase & The Spirit of the Trestle, to be released by Christmas.

Read more at https://books2read.com/ap/RwdkqW/ K-G-Wauthier.